STRAY
DECORUM

STRAY
DECORUM

STORIES

GEORGE SINGLETON

East Baton Rouge Parish Library
Baton Rouge, Louisiana

DZANC
BOOKS

DZANC BOOKS

1334 Woodbourne Street
Westland, MI 48186
www.dzancbooks.org

The characters and events in this book are fictitious. Any similarity to real persons, living or dead, is coincidental and not intended by the author.

STRAY DECORUM

Copyright © 2012, text by George Singleton.

Perfect Attendance, *The Atlantic*; A Man with My Number, *Oxford American*; Vaccination, What Are the Odds?, How Are We Going to Lose This One?, I Feel Like Being Nice Today, *The Georgia Review*; The First to Look Away, Humans Being, *The Kenyon Review*; Where Strangers Claim the Tarnished, *The Cincinnati Review*; I Think I Have What Sharon's Got, *The Rome Review*; Durkheim Looking Down, *Ninth Letter*.

Published 2012 by Dzanc Books
Design by Steven Seighman

ISBN: 9781938103-54-4
First edition: September 2012

ART WORKS.
arts.gov

*michigan council for
arts and cultural affairs*

This project is supported in part by awards from the National Endowment for the Arts and Michigan Council for Arts and Cultural Affairs.

Printed in the United States of America

10 9 8 7 6 5 4 3 2 1

CONTENTS

for Clyde Edgerton, Defender of All Stray Beasts and Humans

STRAY
DECORUM

VACCINATION

My dog Tapeworm Johnson needed legitimate veterinary attention. It had been two years since she received annual shots. I read somewhere that an older dog can overdose on all these vaccinations, and I have found—I share this information with every dog owner I meet—that if you keep your pet away from rabid foxes, raccoons, skunks, bats, and people whose eyes rotate crazy in their sockets, then the chances of your own dog foaming at the mouth diminish drastically. I also believe that dogs don't need microchips embedded beneath their shoulder blades if you keep the dog leashed or in the house, or with the truck windows rolled up when you drive around showing the dog farm animals living in pastures. I brought this up to Dr. Page one time, back four years earlier when Tapeworm Johnson was somewhere between eight and nine. Tapeworm showed up at my door one morning, back when I was married and living in a regular house, her ribs as visible as anything you'd order down at Clem and Lyda's Barbecue Shack off Scenic Highway 11, her paw pads split open from, I assumed, days traveling from wherever her conscienceless owner dropped her off. Tapeworm looked coon or bird dog mostly, though she'd never pointed over the years I've known her, which might explain a stupid hunter letting her loose, without a collar, and so on. Seeing as nothing seemed hopeful in the marriage, I let the dog inside, took her to Dr. Page's ex-colleague Dr. Lloyd Leck—who overdosed on horse tranquilizers awhile back, though people in the community say they were only ostrich tranquilizers seeing as Dr. Leck dealt with the more entrepreneurial ranchers who'd moved in to raise emus, llamas, and the like—and Dr. Leck said the dog had tapeworms. When I had signed in I put "Jane Doe" down for Tapeworm Johnson's name. When we scheduled a second visit for a month later, so the dog could put on weight and get vaccinated for diseases I felt sure got made up by either the American Veterinary Association or the Dog Pill and Serum Manufacturers of the United States, I told the vet to put down "Tapeworm" for a name, what the hell. There are worse possible names. The dog could've been diagnosed with some kind of blocked urethra, or mange.

I have a medical doctor I call Bob. I have an ophthalmologist I call Henry. There's a chiropractor who lives a mile down the road from me in one of those fake log houses built from a kit. I call him Snap-Crackle-Pop when I come across him at the barbecue shack. I refer to professors as teachers, which seems to piss them off. I went to college with our governor, and I call him Fuck-twig now, just as I did back then. So in case anyone thinks I disparage veterinarians—who have to know all the bones of about every animal ever invented, not just the 206 of humans—understand that I call Dr. Page Dr. Page, and before he couldn't take it anymore and offed himself with giant bird tranquilizers, I called Dr. Leck Dr. Leck.

Tapeworm got out of my truck without any aid, and she led me to the clinic's door. One woman sat in the waiting room. She said, "Look, Loretta, you have a friend! Look at the pretty doggie!" in a high-pitched voice normally used by mothers talking to non-verbal babies, or school nurses to special ed first graders who shit their pants and wished that they hadn't. We have a lot of problems these days, and I think that making it a felony to speak in such a manner might eradicate gun violence in the future.

When I signed in I looked down to read "Holly" for the owner's name, and "Loretta" for her dog. Under Reason for Visit Holly had written "toenails." Under Tapeworm's Reason for Visit I wrote down "Change Oil Filter." I figured someone later would see it and then ask Dr. Page if she could check the Jack Russell's oil.

I felt Tapeworm tugging toward Loretta, and when the two dogs' noses touched they wagged their tails. Holly said, "See? They can be friends."

I said, "That's good."

Holly said, "Janie said she's running late. She's back there in surgery. Somebody's dog got shot in the eye. Can you imagine? Janie said it's an emergency, and that she's going to have to amputate the eye." Holly looked normal and friendly enough. She might've been late-thirties, and wore hippie clothing that somehow matched—a thin cotton lavender skirt, a black-and-gray tie-dyed sleeveless blouse, those sandals that cost way too much money because they supposedly offer arch support. If I ever meet a podiatrist I think I'll call him or her Sole Brother or Sole Sister, like that.

I didn't think "amputate" was the correct term for an eyeball, but didn't say anything. Holly wasn't wearing a bra. She didn't shave her armpits, which didn't bother me seeing as the majority of women living on this planet—contrary to popular American Christian belief—didn't shave anywhere, just like most men. Holly had her hair braided three times in long pigtails, which made me scared that she might have been one of those Second Ready people who'd moved into the area, ready in a second for the Second Coming. I figured a Second Ready woman might keep three braids in homage to the Trinity.

"Homage" might not be the correct term. For some reason, I said, "I've known one-eyed dogs and they get around fine. They adapt." I sat down on the bench perpendicular to Holly. Our dogs continued to be friendly.

"I'm Holly and this is Loretta," she said.

"Hey, Holly. I'm Edward Johnson. This is Wanda." Who's going to tell a braless woman you got a dog named Tapeworm? Wanda was my ex-wife's name.

"I've never seen you here," Holly said. "You look like a level-headed person, and I'm always on the lookout for level-headed people. By level-headed, I mean people who love animals and maybe don't record reality TV shows to watch over and over."

I thought about fake-speaking in tongues, but the last time I'd done that as a joke somebody called 9-1-1 and said I underwent an epileptic seizure. This happened at a hardware store when an employee told me that if God wanted a nut and bolt to rust together beyond loosening, then I shouldn't interfere with WD-40.

"It would be kind of a coincidence if you and I came into a vet clinic at the same time more than once," I said.

Holly said, "Ed or Eddie? Or Edward, all the time."

"Edward all the time." I didn't say how Wanda wasn't Wanda all the time. I kind of daydreamed way ahead to Holly calling for Tapeworm—"Wanda! Wanda! Wanda! Come here, Wanda!"—and how I'd have to say how the dog must've lost her hearing.

Holly slid over on her bench in my direction. Tapeworm began panting, and then jumped up beside me. I looked over to the counter and wondered if Dr. Page no longer had a receptionist, then figured that maybe she needed help in the surgery room. Holly said, "Edward. One time I was with my boyfriend—I don't have a man in my life anymore, maybe because of what I'm about to tell you—and I called him Edward out of nowhere, just like in that Led Zeppelin song, you know, about calling out a different guy's name. I didn't even know anyone named Edward back then. Maybe I was having a vision about the future." She smiled. "I got a tattoo of two dung beetles going up the back of my thighs. Maybe one day I'll go to Africa and see some real ones."

I made a mental note to open my dictionary to the "non" section when I got home so maybe I'd finally learn the correct spelling of "non sequitur."

I said, "I got one of a chameleon, but it keeps changing colors and blending right in with my skin."

Dr. Page—maybe every veterinarian in the world—didn't have much taste or imagination in art. She'd gotten a new Norman Rockwell reproduction, her ninth, and it involved a dog and a little boy, like the others. If I were a veterinarian I'd nail Jackson Pollock posters on the wall so people would think, "Well, at least my dog didn't look *that* bad after getting hit out on the highway." There were also rows of Hummel-like dog figurines placed in a shallow figurine display case, *DogFancy* and *Bark* magazines scattered about, and a Canine Weight Guide chart tacked to the door that led into the examination rooms. The TV remained tuned to Animal Planet. An upright plastic holder housed pamphlets for lost pet medical insurance.

"We should go out and get some coffee afterwards," Holly said. "We could drive over to Laurinda's diner. We could sit in the parking lot and let our dogs play together."

I had work to do. I said, "OK."

"We should go out and get a *drink*." Holly looked at her wristwatch. "I'll be in there five minutes. How long will it take for Wanda? As long as she's not getting an operation, let's say fifteen minutes. And then by the time we get to, say, Gus's Place, it'll be eleven. That's not too early. Gus lets dogs come inside."

Dr. Page came out wearing a surgeon's shower cap. She said, "Hey, Edward. Hey, Tapeworm Johnson." She looked at Holly and said, "Come on back. Now, who is this one?"

Holly didn't say anything about the Tapeworm Johnson reference. She drug Loretta into the back. I stood up, let go of Tapeworm's leash, and went outside to look in Holly's car. She drove a VW bug, of course. She left the windows down, which meant—in my mind, at least—it was OK for me to look in her back seat floorboard and glove compartment for pharmaceutical evidence in the way of lithium. I found dog hair. I'm no forensic evidence expert, but I felt pretty sure that I discovered wiry white hair, long copper hair, short black hair, short gray hair, long liver-colored hair, and so on. It didn't all come off of Loretta, is what I'm saying. Did I want to spend an afternoon with a crazy dog woman? That was the question.

I found Grateful Dead cassette tapes and CDs. At first I thought I discovered a roach in the ashtray, but upon smelling it—then eating it—I learned that it, more than likely, ended up being the remnants of a hand-rolled American Spirit cigarette. Did I want to get involved in any way with a woman addicted to the evils of nicotine—like I'd been addicted with cigarettes all the way up until the day after Wanda took off, leaving me alone with Tapeworm?

I wanted to find a grocery list, but I didn't find one. I wanted to find a couple books. If she had a copy of *Don Quixote* I'd've thought that I'd finally met my soul mate. If she had a number of those self-help books, or memoirs written by the brainwashed cast of aliens involved in the Bush administration, I'd've known to've brought a wooden stake along with me to the bar. But I found no reading material. Did I want to sit around in a bar with two dogs that might've been as literate as Holly?

I got out of the Volkswagen, reached the veterinarian's front door, turned around, rolled the windows up all the way on my pickup, and locked both doors so no one could rifle through my belongings. When I got back inside the waiting room I found Tapeworm stretched out on her back legs, eating all the dog biscuits in a bowl between the registration ledger and a doorknob used to tether a dog. Tapeworm turned her head, kept her mouth open, and looked at me with bird-dog eyes that said nothing but "You caught me. I'm sorry, but this is who I am."

I said, "Bad dog, Wanda."

Holly came out with Loretta and right away I noticed not as much clacking on the tile floor. That Dr. Page must be the queen of clipping dog nails, I thought. Holly said to the vet, "I'll see you next week to do the hind nails."

"Okey-dokey," said Dr. Page. She didn't wear the shower cap anymore. To me she said, "Come on back, Edward."

I said, "I owe you some Milk-Bones."

"I'll be at Gus's Place. Come on down there, Edward," Holly said. She leaned in and kissed me on the cheek—Who does that? When did women start kissing strangers on the cheek?—and patted Tapeworm on the head. The dog Loretta licked Tapeworm on the muzzle.

I tried to say, "I might not be there seeing as I have some honeysuckle to gather," but couldn't get it out. I'm no psychologist, but maybe I didn't want Holly to know that I wove baskets for a living. Oh, I can do sweetgrass or river cane or white oak or even pine needle baskets, but my best work—and the ones that sell at craft shows and galleries—is honeysuckle vine. I learned how to do it from my father's sister. She spent time in a nuthouse down in Milledgeville.

Tapeworm led me into the examination room. Dr. Page kept a frightening poster up on one wall of dog eyeball scenarios, like glaucoma in various stages. I didn't like it. On another wall she kept a poster of a normal dog's alimentary canal, above a poster of dog mouths with tooth and gum diseases.

I said, "Tapeworm's fine in all ways except the shots needed."

I'd had dreams about Dr. Page, I have to admit. Who has dreams about his veterinarian? I wondered if my *dog* had veterinarian dreams. I know that we always see dogs paddling their paws and whining in their sleep, and we say, "Hey, the dog's dreaming about chasing rabbits." Maybe they're not. Maybe our dogs dream of running away from veterinarians.

I had dreams of Dr. Page wearing, you know, more of a traditional French maid's outfit than the blue pants suit that she always wore. In one dream Dr. Page took out a special metal comb and ran it through my hair as I froze on the metal examination table. In another, Dr. Page announced, "Heartworm!" like that.

"What a day. Goddamn," she said to me while checking Tapeworm's coat.

I wondered how many veterinarians, percentage-wise, weren't Christians and used the Lord's name in vain, as I felt that they should seeing as too many people abused God's supposed creatures. I said, "It's OK, Tapeworm," and lifted her to the table. To the vet I said, "Is it really 'amputate' an eyeball?"

"That woman's insane, you know," Dr. Page said. "Did you have enough time to talk to her? Did you gather that she's crazy?"

I shrugged. I shook my head. "What?"

"Absolutely out of her mind. I'm scared of her, to be honest. If I could ever find a receptionist again who could be pleasant to people, I'd pay double just to have someone in here with me at all times."

What kind of segue did I have to offer? I said, "My aunt spent some time in a mental institution in Milledgeville, Georgia. Nowadays they'd say she was bipolar, but back then she was known mostly as completely nuts by people in my family."

Dr. Page listened to Tapeworm's heart and lungs with a stethoscope. She checked her ears and said, "I bet your aunt wasn't convinced that government officials try to embed microchips into her."

I said, "No," not making a connection between Holly and microchips. I thought of my aunt. We used to go visit her in the hospital when I was a kid. She called my father—her brother—Elvis Presley. She tried to strangle my mother one time, screaming out, "I am not a vessel for your sticks and stones, I am not a vessel for your sticks and stones!" That might've been the last time we visited as a group. My mother called her sister-in-law a "basket case" over and over to anyone who'd listen. I didn't get along very well with my mother—she forever contradicted Dad, and belittled him whenever possible, bringing up how no one in my father's family could be trusted, what with the crazy gene—and maybe that's what drove me toward basket weaving, out of meanness, shortly after I graduated college with a degree in journalism, and shortly after my father shoved a garden hose in his muffler and led the business end into the cracked open window of his Buick. I said to Dr. Page, "Are you kidding me?" and tried to make eye contact without imagining her in a French maid's outfit.

"That wasn't even her dog," Dr. Page said. "She goes around picking up strays, getting them shots, then dumps them back out. Or she offers to bring her neighbors' dogs in to get their toenails clipped, whatever. And then she gets in here and asks that I scan her body for computer chips she's convinced have been implanted by the FBI." She picked up her handheld scanner. "I scan the stray to make sure it's not a lost dog, and then I scan Holly."

I said, "Man." I couldn't think of anything else to say, and I knew ahead of time what my next dream would involve with my veterinarian.

Dr. Page replaced the scanner and picked up a syringe. "This is for rabies and parvo, plus a new strain of canine polio that's going around." At least that's what I heard. It was something that I didn't believe really struck down dogs. Tapeworm didn't flinch, though I held her muzzle shut just in case. Dr. Page said, "How old is Tapeworm now?"

"Between twelve and twenty," I said.

"What a good dog," she said. Then, in that voice that's used by people who need to live where my father's sister spent most of her adult life, Dr. Page said, "Who's a good girl? Yes! Yes! Who's a good girl? That's right—you're a good girl."

I cradled my dog and pulled her down to the floor. I said, "Damn." I meant, Damn—you just ruined my respect for you. I said, "You ever found a microchip on Holly?"

My vet laughed. "Sometimes I go *beep* when I'm scanning her, just for fun. No. From what I understand, back when you could just park in front of an airport and walk in even if you weren't flying anywhere, Holly used to walk through the metal detectors. She used to take off her jewelry, you know, and walk through in hopes of setting the thing off."

Dr. Page touched my chest. Well, no, she pushed me out of the examination room, in a way to let me know gently that her time with Tapeworm was over. I walked back to the waiting room with my dog. Dr. Page took a different turn, and ended up on the other side of the counter. She said, "Is Tapeworm on heartworm medication?"

I said, "She's inside the house or with me. She never gets in a rabid animal situation. I have a privacy fence."

"Mosquitoes transmit heartworm, Edward. Mosquitoes can pretty much find ways to buzz over fences."

I felt like an idiot, of course. I said, "Oh. Well, then, I guess she's not."

"You need some protection, I promise. Especially now, what with the rain."

I said OK—she might've been flirting with me, what with that "You need some protection" comment—and Dr. Page turned to pick up a year's worth of Heartgard Plus tablets. She said, "Shots and checkup come to a hundred bucks. The heartworm protection's eighty." She typed on her computer. "Let's call it an even one-eighty."

I hadn't spent $180 on my own health care in the previous decade. I said, "We need veterinary health care reform."

"Yeah, yeah, yeah," Dr. Page said. She said, "We need to make sure there's mental health coverage for that new girlfriend of yours, if you ask me. And for other people who've been in my life, I suppose."

I thought maybe she made reference to Dr. Leck's accidental overdose of horse tranquilizers. "You looking for a partner?" I meant, of course, "Are you looking to bring another vet in here to help you out?"

Dr. Page said, "I'm not a lesbian, Edward."

Back in my dreams! I thought. I said, "That's not what I meant," and handed over nine twenties. That's the thing about basket weavers. We have cash, always.

"Have fun with Holly. Hope to see you again one day."

I wanted to talk more, but the door opened and a man came in with a limping beautiful mutt. I knew the guy. I saw him sometimes talking to himself down at Laurinda's, or I saw him driving slowly with his face dangerously close to his windshield.

Dr. Page said, "Hey, Stet, what's up?"

He said, "Someone's setting traps around."

What should a divorced basket weaver do when tempted by a microchip-believing hippie woman intent on drinking before noon? I said to Tapeworm, "You want to go to a bar? Does Tapeworm want to go for a ride to the bar?" but I swear to fucking God I said it all in a normal voice, as if I might be talking to a friend from college or my crazy aunt.

Tapeworm Johnson said nothing. Tapeworm Johnson sat upright on the truck's bench seat and looked straight out the windshield, as good found stray bird dogs are wont to do.

I drove down Scenic Highway 11 past my driveway, and past Looper's landscape rock operation, and past Laurinda's until, finally, I took a couple macadam roads and turned into Gus's Place. I tried not to go to this particular bar on the Saluda River very often. One time I showed up there and three men hid behind the counter, saying that someone had a gun. Another time I went in and a homeless drifter insisted that she was one of the premiere book critics in the country. For the record, I would rather be in a bar with a possible gun toter on the loose than a drifter book critic. I remember telling Tapeworm that day, "Remind me to pay my tab immediately should someone next to me at the bar ever use the term 'postmodern.'"

I parked next to Holly's VW, the only car in the gravel parking spots. Inside, Gus stood behind the counter, mouth dropped open, staring at Holly. She'd leashed Loretta to one of the stools, which Loretta tipped over and dragged behind her in order to sniff my dog's butt.

"Haven't you ever ordered a scotch and Mr. Pibb?" Holly asked me.

Gus didn't close his mouth or move his mouth visibly, though his eyes shifted to me. I said, "I can't say that I've ever gotten to that point." To Gus I said, "I'll have whatever you have on draft that's not light."

"Sanity arrives," Gus said. "I don't even carry Mr. Pibb. Do they still make it?"

Holly scooted a stool a few inches my way and told me to sit down. She said, "No, but I have a stockpile, and I thought maybe you did, too. We've been to the vet's. We met at the vet's office. What a romantic story this'll be one day!"

"Tell your dog not to drag my stool around," Gus said. I got up, told my own dog to sit. She did, and I righted Loretta's stool and slid it over to the bar counter.

To Gus, Holly said, "Well, then, surprise me. But I can't drink beer. It has to be liquor, and it can't be straight."

Gus said, "You got it." He turned around and stared at his bottles, picked out the vodka, then turned around and stared at his mixers in a cold box.

No music played. The walls were bare, though squares and rectangles of a different shade proved that Gus, at one time, kept something nailed up which, I would bet, weren't Norman Rockwell reproductions. "All my dogs used to start barking at five o'clock every morning, wanting to go outside," Holly said. "Unless it was raining. If it rained, they all acted as if they didn't need to use the bathroom. So you know what I did? I bought one of those noise machines where you can click on to whales pinging, or ocean surf, birds of the Amazon, and *rain*. I put it on a timer in the kitchen, so it goes off at four o'clock every morning until seven. The dogs haven't figured it out yet. They sure don't whine and bark anymore until about five minutes after the machine clicks off. How about that? Pretty ingenious, huh?"

Gus placed a martini glass in front of Holly. He said, "Vodka and Jarritos. It's some kind of mango soda all the Guatemalans order. Cheers."

Holly said "Cheers," and I thought about lifting my glass but I said, "That's not your dog," and pointed at Loretta.

Holly downed her poor man's screwdriver as if it were a shooter. She held her chin down to her throat and grimaced. Gus wiped his hands on what may have been the first bar towel ever made. It looked like a nicotine-stained tatter of cheesecloth. He said, "I normally wait until noon," and pulled a can of Schlitz out of the cooler.

Holly said, "Hooooo! That went straight through me. Can you watch my dog? I have to pee."

I nodded.

And then, of course, I went through her pocketbook that she left on the bar. I found a flask, a pack of that rolling tobacco, some papers, and two rolls of quarters. She had a skein of uncompromised two-dollar scratch-off tickets. Holly had some kind of Friend of the World Wildlife Fund membership card, and another from PETA.

Gus said, "Do you know her?" in a whisper.

I said, "Do you?"

"She's been here before. One time she brought in a snapping turtle, lodged in one of those cat litter boxes with a top that snaps on. Scared the shit out of my customers. That thing kept shooting its head out, like a foot-long pecker."

I said, "The vet says she's nuts."

I found no driver's license, Social Security card, credit card, or passport. Who doesn't have those things, outside of people on the lam, children under the age of fifteen, or illegal aliens who sit around drinking Jarritos mango soda in their spare time?

Gus cleared his throat. I understood it to be the international signal for "She's coming back out of the restroom."

I shuffled everything back into her purse, looked down at the dogs, said, "Hey, Loretta," and noticed that the dog didn't look up at me. *Her name's not Loretta*, I thought.

"Sure she's my dog," Holly said upon her return. "It's my dog. Did that bitch Janie Page say I brought in dogs that weren't mine? Why would I do that? She's hated me since I started going there. I'd go somewhere else, but the next vet's something like thirty miles away, you know. She's hates me! You wouldn't believe how many women hate me!"

My ex-wife used to say the same thing. That's what made me so surprised when she left for someone named Michele, before I learned that it was someone named *Michel*, a French-Canadian guy who'd come down south in order to write a book on folk artists.

Gus said, "You want another? If you drink them that fast, I can make you a triple and put it in a regular glass like his."

Tapeworm Johnson barked twice for some reason and began panting. She looked at Loretta, then chewed toward the base of her own tail.

Holly said, "Hell, man, if you have a tumbler I'll take a double-triple. I've finished my work for the day. I've done my job, for the most part."

I couldn't tell if she wanted me to ask what she did for a living, or if I was supposed to comprehend that taking someone else's dog to a vet, getting ten of its toenails clipped, and having her own neck area scanned for microchips constituted a full day's activities. So I was happy when Gus asked, "What kind of work is it that you got, lets you be done before noon? I want that job, unless it's third shift."

I said, "Me, too," just to be one of the boys. I didn't even want the flexibility of being a basket weaver, to be honest. In another life I kind of wanted to be an astronaut, seeing as by then they'd have most of the kinks worked out.

"Oh, you know. I do what I do," Holly said. "I've been a couple things in corporate America, and then I got out before the bubble burst. Right now I'm helping some people raise money and awareness toward the plight of the Nepalese. I'm a fundraiser. If I feel like working in the middle of the night, I call potential donors in Japan. I have an altitude training tent that I sleep in and everything, just in case I get a call and need to fly to the Himalayas on short notice."

Gus said nothing. I stared at Holly way too long, trying to gather it all in. I said, "I've seen those things. It's like what a bubble boy lives in. Hey, what's your last name, anyway?"

Holly said, "I'm down to fifteen percent oxygen."

On my way to the men's room an hour later I thought about how Holly might've killed some brain cells. I had seen a documentary one time about some mountain bikers readying themselves for the Leadville 100 out in Colorado. They'd slept in an altitude training tent for three months. None of them could tie their shoes or figure out a zipper, much less sing the National Anthem or name two rivers east of the Mississippi. They could ride bikes up steep inclines, though. I thought, Will it be immoral to have sex with a woman who's only using fifteen percent of her brain? I thought, As bad as corporate America's doing, I'm glad Holly isn't involved with it now, only using fifteen percent oxygen.

I thought all kinds of things. I wondered how come I tuned Holly out with all her talk of Sherpas between my first and fifth beer, and obsessed with how Wanda would have said, "I told you so, I told you so," like a mantra, should had she entered the bar. I daydreamed about Dr. Page showing up not wearing scrubs, and telling me what a good, faithful friend I'd been for

Tapeworm. I thought about how I couldn't get so drunk that I got talked into donating a series of honeysuckle vine baskets so the indigenous people of Nepal could carry them atop their heads like indigenous people. I read the graffiti in the men's room and wondered if whoever wrote "The joke's in your hand, Stet," referred to the same man Dr. Page greeted at her office as I left.

I came back to the bar proper to find Gus alone. Out the window I could see Holly's Volkswagen not parked next to my truck. Gus stood leaning over the drink box, wringing his hands with the bar towel. "Where the fuck's my dog?" I said. I walked straight out the door and ran to my truck. Gus followed. I yelled, "Which way did that woman go?"

Gus said, "She paid the tab."

I yelled out, "Tapeworm, Tapeworm, Tapeworm!" in the hope that she'd merely gone out the door, that she went looking for me.

"She took both dogs," Gus said. "She paid the tab and left me a big old tip, and then she said she needed to walk the dogs. I heard her car start up and the door close, but I wasn't thinking."

I didn't want to cry in front of Gus. I got in my truck, and drove way too fast and impaired away from the direction where I lived. Wanda leaving me was one thing, but losing Tapeworm would've sent me to Gus's Place daily. I rolled down the windows and yelled for my dog about every fifty yards.

When the road finally came to a four-way stop sign I pulled over and listened for the remnants of a puttering VW engine. When I called a 9-1-1 operator and explained the situation— unstable woman who steals dogs, thinks there's a microchip implanted between her shoulder blades, fundraiser for the impoverished goat herders of Nepal—the man on the other end informed me that it was a felony to misuse the nine-eleven system, but I felt pretty sure that it was only a misdemeanor.

I made a U-turn, slowed down to see no one parked at the

bar, and continued until I got to Dr. Page's vet clinic to see if she had this Holly's woman's phone number and address. The lot was empty. I'm not too proud to say that I opened my glove compartment, found some old paper napkins from Captain Del Kell's Galley Bell, wiped my eyes and blew my nose.

Tapeworm sat in the waiting room alone, the handle of her leash looped around that doorknob attached to the counter.

I said, "Goddamn, I'm glad you're here," and bent down to hug my dog. Dr. Page came out of the back. Maybe I blurted out some blubbering sounds. I said, "That Holly woman stole my dog."

Dr. Page said, "What're you doing back here?" She reached down and scratched Tapeworm's jowl. "Did you forget something?"

I said, "I'm serious. That Holly woman stole Tapeworm when I went to take a leak."

My veterinarian shook her head. She looked at me as if I made everything up. Then she walked over to one of the end tables and said, "You really ought to reconsider getting a chip for Tapeworm, and some of this lost pet medical insurance."

I untethered my dog. Later, I would blame my irrational thought processes either on too many beers in too short a time, or from just *thinking about* an oxygen deprivation tent. "I might only be a honeysuckle vine basket weaver who supplies a number of arts and crafts galleries in the South, but I know a scam when I see one. You hire out Holly to pretend to be crazy, then she kidnaps dogs and you get some kind of kickback from the pet insurance and microchip companies. You can't fool me. You're not going to get this by on me."

Dr. Page didn't react one way or the other immediately. In future dreams, I would see her standing in my bedroom, wearing scrubs, acting nonplussed as a woven trivet. She would shake her head one way, her index finger working in tandem. I would feel guilty, as I did standing there with my dog's leash handle in one hand and a pamphlet for the lost pet insurance in the other.

I could've walked out indignantly. I could've asked for Dr.

Page to forget veterinarian-client privileges and give me Holly's address and phone number so I could run her down and seek justice. Instead, I stood there, frozen, my dog Tapeworm wagging her tail ready to go for another ride, and wondered if this type of situation finally caused my first vet to overdose.

"Maybe crazy Holly's like that Christo artist who covers things up, then unveils them anew. Maybe she wanted you to realize what you'd taken for granted in a pet," Dr. Page said.

I was stunned. How could a woman awash in Norman Rockwell prints understand the avant-garde work of Christo? I asked her if she'd like to meet somewhere, like Gus's bar, when she got off work. I couldn't think of anything else to say, and knew that no apology would work.

Dr. Page said it might be best if I leave.

I could not make eye contact. I felt empty, empty. When I asked my dog's veterinarian if she could sell me some horse tranquilizers, I tried to make it come off as a joke. I might've said, "Corporate America." I might've thought, "Choke collar."

WHAT ARE THE ODDS?

WE DIDN'T KNOW THAT our dogsitter smoked so much dope, until Vina and I returned from an old-school Las Vegas trip much lighter in the savings account—sporting tattoos that meant something to us individually only—and found our wooden floors spotless and glistening. I'd turned fifty a month earlier. Between my actual birthday and Vina's planned trip out west I read twenty-one separate how-to books about the sport of blackjack. Everything's symbolic and numerology-ridden for me, I hate to admit. So what? I count cars on my way to the Slip-In store and use that number daily when choosing my Cash 5, Pick 3, Mega Match 6, or Powerball numbers, unless I need to bastardize the situation. The Slip-In's 1.7 miles away from my house. (Guess how many times I've used the numeral 17, or 1, or 7, or 8, seeing as one plus seven equals eight?) One time I passed the funeral of what must've been a long-time republican state senator seeing as I pulled off on the berm as is rightly southern etiquette and counted 234 cars, most of which didn't get good gas mileage according to all those consumer magazines. That's why and how I deduced that it was a politician. Anyway, as everyone knows, there's not any kind of daily, bi-weekly, or special education lottery with a "234" as one of the viable options to pick. So on that day I played a slew of games and chose numbers 2, 3, 4, 23, 34, 24, 43, 42, 5, 7, 6, 32, and 9. I didn't win anything. I didn't even catch one number on the Pick 3, or two on the Cash 5. Some days it's like that, trying to outguess televised bouncing balls. Other days it's night, and nothing but irrational behavior comes this way after dusk which, I suppose, is what causes dogsitters to light up and hold it in.

"What did you do, wax the floor or something?" I said to Josh when we dropped our suitcases in the kitchen. I looked out to the den/dining room/living room/entertainment room that only accounted for about six hundred square feet but had immaculate Lay'N'Snap fake wood flooring that Vina and I installed ourselves three years earlier when we realized that our thirteen year old dog Murray had peed on about every square inch of the carpet. Murray had showed up in our yard already fixed, but I believed that the veterinarian might've accidentally jiggled the dog's major urethra nerve along the way somehow. Our vet told us that Murray appeared to be part Boston terrier, part beagle, and part Ivy League graduate judging from his extraordinary, prominent underbite. No matter his lineage, the dog could go outside, pee two minutes on a fire ant mound, then come inside and lift his leg on the couch, the middle of the room, my foot.

Josh attended graduate school. Neither Vina nor I remembered how Josh became our dog sitter, or how his name filtered down as the most viable of job applicants. Something about Vina's boss having a sister who went through a divorce years earlier and thus having a child who got brought up soft-hearted for strays. Anyway, Josh had gone to one of those experimental colleges where students made up their own majors. He held a bachelor's degree in Depressive Poets and a minor in Famous Boy Scouts, or something like that. Afterwards he couldn't get a job—imagine that—then came home to live with his mother and work on a low-residency master's degree a couple weeks out of the year. When Josh showed up for us to meet him I didn't quite listen to his previous work experience. He'd worked at a coffee shop, evidently, but that was it.

"Yeah, I swept and mopped the floor," Josh said.

Vina walked into the bathroom to find rubbing alcohol. She'd been trying to pick off the remnants of one strip of adhesive tape from her tattoo-gauze ever since downing two vodka tonics and jerking off the bandage in one motion. She first ripped off both pieces, on her ankle, in order to apply A&D Ointment right there at the blackjack table at the Golden Nugget where the dealer'd shown a face card about thirteen times in a row while my two cards always added up to twelve, thirteen, or fourteen. None of those books mentioned how this could happen in a six, eight, or fifteen shoe of decks. I should've called up someone from Guinness to witness this entire spectacle just in case I could've made it into their *World Records* annual.

Vina came out and said hey to Josh. She yelled out, "Come here, Murray! Come here, boy! Hurry, Murray! Come on! You want to go for a ride? It's time for dinner! You want some curry, Murray? Come here, furry Murray! Do you want a slurry, Murray?" like she did most days when she came home and Murray slept probably dreaming about the old carpet.

But our dog didn't come limping up to greet us. No matter how hearing-impaired he'd become, enough yelling had him at least running into the room, even if he ended up staring at the floor lamp or fireplace. Vina said, "Don't make me worry, Murray."

"I fucked up," Josh said. He wore plaid Bermuda shorts and a T-shirt with a slogan that read For Whom the Bell Jar Tolls. He shook visibly, which I realized later might've been difficult for someone who hits a bong hourly. "I'm sorry. I'll pay y'all back. I used the money you paid me to pay for my car insurance. But the next time I get paid I'll send y'all the money you paid me to stay here."

Vina said, "Where's my dog?" She looked at me instead of Josh. This would, somehow, become my fault.

Josh said, "I called up this girl Kelsey I knew in college. She was supposed to come over here, you know, and visit. Kelsey's living back home with her parents, until she either finds a job or goes back to grad school. Anyway, I realized that I probably needed to take a shower before she showed up, and then I couldn't figure out how y'all's bathtub became a shower. What's with that tub back there?"

Vina stepped toward me and said, "Where's the dog?"

Josh held up his palm. I wanted him to hurry up because I needed to go to the bank and turn in some savings bonds. "I turned on the tub, man, and Murray *freaked out*. I guess he thought I was going to throw him in there. So I let him outside. And then my cell phone rang and Kelsey was lost. No, wait—she called saying that she was going to be late. And I told her that was all right. Then I guess I fell asleep out there in the sun room, you know. The next thing I knew, she called saying she was kind of lost."

I said, "Do you steal money from your mother? How do you pay for pot? I know that it costs a ton of money these days."

See that? See what I did? Josh hadn't said anything about rolling a joint, or taking a hit from the bong up until this point. I made what might be called a "calculated inference risk." I think I came across the term in one of those blackjack books.

"Yeah, man, I'm sorry. You're right. I got all smoked up, and then the next thing you know I walked into the den and saw what I thought was a big piss by Murray. I'm talking it was all over the place. *Then* I remembered leaving the tub on. I went in and turned off the water, and drained the tub. I got all the towels and cleaned it up, plus I got that wet-dry vac out of the garage."

Vina said, "That's not a wet-dry vacuum cleaner."

So did I. We don't have any kind of running video camera in the house, but I'm pretty sure I said, "not a wet-dry" before my wife did.

Josh shrugged and shook his head sideways. "Man. Y'all are lucky I didn't get electrocuted."

————

Sometimes I used to pull the dollar bills out of my wallet and use those numbers. For example, if I had a bill number 13147381, on a Cash 5 I'd pick 13 and 14, surely. But then I might've taken the 73 and 81, and added them up together for a 10 and a 9. Then I'd have to maybe throw in a 3, seeing as there were three ones in that long number. Eventually those numbers would show up and make me a millionaire or more, understand. The one thing I think about more than anything is, What if I die and my favorite numbers show up the next day? What does that mean?

Here's what it means: No God. There are people out there who think God equals mathematics, that it's all a matter of numbers. There's some kind of infinity symbol that looks like the numeral 8 on its side. It's what Vina got tattooed on her ankle. I can tell you this: Walking between the tattoo parlor on East Fremont and the El Cortez casino where dealers use a single deck so it's impossible to bust 22 eight or ten times in a row, and between the El Cortez and the Golden Nugget, and between the Golden Nugget and the McCarran International Airport, and then all the time flying to South Carolina, Vina had exactly *zero* New Agers, physicists, automobile designers, or Buddhist monks point at her ankle and say, "Infinity!" On the other hand, I couldn't have counted how many men and women said, "Aw-ight—Dale Earnhardt, Jr," or "Aw-ight—Little E," or "Aw-ight, Junior," or "Hey, Little Dale's number 88 now. You missing a eight," and so on. Vina had no clue what anyone meant until I told her how there was a stock car driver, et cetera. Months later, long after Murray returned, when somebody at the Slip-In held up eight fingers—sometimes because they didn't have thumbs—Vina yelled, "Aw-ight! Infinity! Endless cycle!"

I never understood why she chose that particular tattoo. The only people who thought it didn't stand for a number painted on the side of a car thought it was a ribbon in remembrance of breast cancer, soldiers in Operation Desert Storm, soldiers in the second invasion of Iraq that didn't appear to have a code name, lung cancer, or local missing children.

Me, I got Dave the Tattoo Artist to drill my skin with a giant black bull's eye. When Vina asked what it stood for I didn't tell her that it should make me a better target for when she fired emasculating missiles my way. I didn't say, "You know, Melvina, I'm sorry that I don't live up to your expectations." I didn't say, "Well, this mandala-of-sorts on my arm represents the pummeling I take daily for not being the regular fucking nine-to-five businessman you should've married."

I said, "It's kind of like a clock with no arms."

Vina said, "That makes no sense. Anything round is a clock with no arms. Never mind. Hey, we should call Josh and make sure he and Murray are okay."

Later on—it's always later on, isn't it?—I thought about how a clock with no arms could also represent infinity.

We called. Josh answered. He said, "All is well. I've been working on a poem all day. And my friend Kelsey's coming over, if that's all right. I'm going to bake up some of those potatoes y'all have in the freezer."

I said, "Murray hasn't bitten you on the face or anything, has he? Sometimes if you try to pick him up, he'll bite you on the face."

"No sir. He's fine." Then Josh said he had to go. He said the oven had reached temperature.

Standing there with him in our living room, with my dog missing and my wife frantic, I realized that, had I not called, our house would've been flooded more so, then probably burned to the ground from the unwatched oven. I said, "Well, you're not electrocuted, so that's beside the point."

Vina kept calling for our dog. She marched throughout the house, opening closet doors. Her voice turned to screeches on par with a dog whistle. I didn't want Vina to return with a crying face. When I quit my last real job abruptly, I made a point not to ever see my wife cry again. I don't want to say that that's what kept me from ever seeking lawful employment again, but maybe subconsciously I knew that if I got another job I would only threaten my boss, and the outcome would be my coming home to announce, "Well, I quit," like that. I imagine that I suffer from some kind of Administrator-Hate Syndrome. I'm sure there's a more technical, specific term.

I was a social worker. I'm a sociologist, broadly speaking.

"Murray's outside somewhere," Josh said. "I mean, I don't think he opened the back door and came inside and has been hiding from me for two days." Josh went on to tell us about how he walked up and down the road, checking with our neighbors who lived three-fourths of a mile in one direction and a quarter-mile in the other. In between and behind us were woods, sloping down to a wide creek that fed the Middle Saluda River, which fed the Saluda, which fed a river mid-state, which flowed into the Atlantic Ocean eventually.

Vina ran outside yelling our dog's name. She disappeared into the pines. I kind of caught myself daydreaming about Murray on a wooden raft, wearing a sailor's cap, floating down to the coast. I said, "Are you an idiot or something?" to my dogsitter.

Josh said, "Can I get you to jumpstart my car? I freaked out so much about the dog running off that I tried to drive away right before y'all showed up. But my battery's dead. I think I might've left the lights on."

I could hear my wife calling out for Murray. The dog couldn't hear that well, and I made a pact with myself not to point this out to Vina, whether the dog turned up or not. I said to Josh, "Listen, Vina went that way," and pointed. "I'm going to take the road down to the Slip-In, and you go up the road that way." I said, "You get the leash in case you find him and he doesn't trust walking back home with you."

Josh said, "Okay. Oh, wait." He walked back into the guest bedroom and came back with Murray's collar. "I took his collar off. He kind of starting coughing that first night and I thought he choked." He handed me the collar. On it were two tags—one proving that he'd been vaccinated, the other a silver metal dog bone with our address and telephone number. "I fucked up."

I thought about punching my dogsitter, but remembered what happened to me six months earlier when I punched out a man caught for beating his wife, child, and neighbor's child down at a trailer park on the outskirts of a mill village, back when I worked.

I didn't find Murray. On my walk I came across three separate men picking up aluminum cans. The first man lugged two filled Hefty bags. The second guy had a plastic grocery bag with what the first one must've missed, and the third man looked confused as to why no one littered anymore. I asked all three if they'd seen Murray, or any kind of dog, during their travels. None had. The first man said he saw a coyote one time. The second guy said he knew me, and asked if I had any cans at home I'd like to give up. The third man kept saying how he wasn't a registered sexual predator, that if you got on the internet it was only a man who looked like him, et cetera.

When I got to the Slip-In I realized that I should've asked the first and second guy how many cans they'd picked up so I could use those numbers on a lottery ticket or three. I thought, I wish I'd've brought a cell phone in case Vina found Murray while I wasn't but a hundred yards from the house.

"Hey there, Smiley," Sharilyn said when I walked in. She didn't know my real name. Sharilyn called me Smiley because she said, maybe ten years earlier, that she'd already used up the other six dwarves' names on regular customers. I never told her that Smiley didn't live alongside Grumpy, Sleepy, Sneezy, et al. I wondered what local person she tabbed Doc. "Where you been? We 'bout went out of business what with you being missing." Sharilyn wore her gray hair piled atop her head like a cumulous cloud.

I nodded and smiled. I'd already scanned the plate glass windows out front for Found Dog posters. There were nine lost pit bulls, and one that read "Thank you to everybody who give us donations after our trailer blowed up," signed by a couple named Slim and Sandy. They'd drawn a confederate flag off to the side. Another sign advertised an upcoming yard sale that featured baseball cards, figurines, plates, matchbox cars, and holiday glitter pine cones.

I said, "Hey, Sharilyn. Hey, my old dog's run off. You know that dog of mine Murray sometimes I got in the car? He's missing. There been anyone come in here saying they found a dog by any chance?"

Sharilyn shook her head. She said, "Josh lost your dog? Damn. I wouldn't want to be him right now."

Of course I stared at Sharilyn for a few seconds before I said, "How the hell do you know my dogsitter?" I didn't say anything about how she knew his real name but didn't know mine. I said, "Yeah."

"I had to order more Zigzags and Jobs because of that boy. Either he smoked a lot of weed, or he can't roll for shit, one or the other. Goddang. How many papers is in a pack of one point fives? They must be a good eighteen, twenty-six, or thirty-two, last time I checked."

I repeated those numbers in my head. What odd choices to use, I thought. I said, "Hey, let me get one of those Cash 5 cards to fill out."

Sharilyn handed one over, plus a short pencil best used on a golf course. Someone came in the store and asked Sharilyn for directions to the fat lighter forest. She said, "You just keep driving thataway until you smell it like kerosene." I gave her back my picks, plus two dollars. Sharilyn said, "Hey, Smiley, I don't want to rub it in or nothing, but have you ever won?"

I lifted up my sleeve. I showed her my new tattoo. "Things are going to change," I said, like a fool.

On the walk back home I didn't repeat the mantra I normally said—though usually driving with Murray—asking God to pick whatever numbers I'd chosen when the ping-pong balls shot up pneumatically at 6:59 P.M. each night on the three local networks Vina and I received. No, I walked home the 1.7 miles only hoping that my dog returned. How sad is it to lose an old mostly-deaf-and-blind dog who got confused? How guilty would we feel for turning fifty and thinking we needed tattoos, only to find out our dog died during this arbitrary vacation?

I picked up two cans that had either been missed by the three scavengers or thrown out while I dealt with Sharilyn. One of them was a Pabst Blue Ribbon. That was fifteen letters. The other happened to be a Colt 45.

My wife held our dog on the front porch. Murray appeared to have been in a bramble thicket of beggar's lice at some point in his adventure, and he squinted one eye. Maybe he came across a cat, or underground yellow jacket nest. The pads of his paws bled slightly. I'm no veterinarian or expert on friction, but Murray must've spent some time traveling on asphalt or gravel. My wife said, "He wasn't that far away. I found him sitting erect, staring at a tree stump." To the dog she said in a sing-songy voice, "You thought you sat in front of your daddy, didn't you, Murray. You mistook a tree stump for your daddy."

I caught myself thinking, If I win the big lottery I'm going to kidnap Murray and move away. I thought, If she only sees me as a stump, then I need to be a good tree and leave. I said, "Man. I can't tell you how bad I would feel if..."

"Where's Josh?" Vina asked.

I pointed in the direction I'd last seem him walking. "I'll get in the car and go hunt him down," I said. "Then I have to jumpstart his car."

My wife shook her head. "Let him walk back. First off, maybe it'll be something he'll remember next time he works for someone. Someone who will not be us." She took Murray off of her lap. He walked toward the wall and stared at it. "Plus, he said he's a poet. It'll give him something to write about."

I stuck out my hand to help Vina off the stoop. "Listen," I said. "Let's put Murray back inside. Let's put him in the bedroom and when Josh comes back we'll act like we never found the dog. I need you to give me a heads up when Josh gets back, too. I'm going to look through his stuff."

I don't have any sociological or cultural anthropological research data to back my claim, but I'd be willing to bet that most wives—especially ones tattooed with New Age infinity signs—might say, "You can't go rifling through the dogsitter's bags." Vina said, "Good idea. See if he really sent off all that money we gave him to his insurance company. If he didn't, take back a hundred dollars. That's a fair trade for Murray's troubles lost in the woods. Take two hundred. Take it all. We might end up having to fight mold and mildew because of the flood."

I just wanted to find his pot, to be honest. I thought maybe after I got his car back charged and him on the road, maybe Vina and I could pass a joint between us, like in the old days. When I first started working for the Department of Social Services and Vina worked as a paralegal for an attorney who specialized in defending DUI and simple possession clients—this was when we were maybe twenty-five to thirty-nine years old—it was impossible not to come home and hit a pipe or drink a pitcher of martinis. How could we not? You spend all day listening to people talk about their problems, all of which either center around or at least bump up against controlled and uncontrolled substances, and there wasn't much else to do outside of throwing two frozen pizzas in the oven and working hard to erase each day's stories and the faces that they came out of.

In the guest bedroom I found Josh's duffel bag wide open. His dirty clothes lay scattered throughout the room and the distinct odor of what I thought might be old Murray urine emanated from the closet's closed louvered doors. For a good couple seconds I forgot that Vina had found our dog already, and I imagined the hero status I would receive for whipping open the door to expose poor sad trapped Murray, dog ankle deep in his own pee. Maybe that lapse of remembrance worked as a sign that I shouldn't return to the Land of Toke, I don't know. Anyway, I found most of our towels, thoroughly wet, balled up on the floor, reeking.

I left them there. I wanted Josh to come back so I could say, "Do you smell that? I smell something," kind of like how I used to toy with men and women living in meth lab trailers.

In his bag I found six rolled joints and a handful of black and white snapshots of Josh, fist to chin, obviously practicing for any book jacket author photos he saw a need for in the future. I found the three one-hundred dollar bills I'd paid the guy to watch our dog, get the mail, and flood our house over a six-day period. I set the pot aside and checked out two large, zippered inner pockets. There I found two rolls of silver dollars, some two dollar silver certificates, some wooden nickels, a rabbit's foot, and my lucky Case knife—all things that I kept in a fireproof box hidden in a bottom desk drawer beneath a false bottom.

He didn't try to swipe any of my wife's valuables. I'm talking she had 24-carat jewelry and diamonds the size of white oak acorns, inherited from women on her mother's side of the family who tended to marry below their station. Vina hid her valuables attached behind a tapestry-looking thing she'd woven herself a few years back when she thought adult education classes at the closest two-year college might do us some good. She took weaving. Her end product came out so ugly that any burglar this side of being legally blind wouldn't think to steal it, or even lift it away from the wall to check behind it.

Me, I took a four-week whittling class. I have a handmade set of toothpicks to prove it. And then I went on to carve a bunch of walking sticks that sell for more money than I ever made asking parents if they stuck their children's hands to open flames. And I carved odd scary masks that buyers down at the flea market might or might not think are genuine Cherokee warpath accessories.

I said, "Fucking dogsitter. You fucking little poet fucker," out loud. I said, "Come on back here, boy."

Vina made me put the Louisville Slugger down after I'd told her the story. She said, "Maybe there's a reason why we have only one dog and no children."

All of this took place, by the way, long before sunset. My wife and I left Las Vegas at 11:35 at night, flew to Atlanta, sat around for a couple hours, got confused because I couldn't remember if I changed my wristwatch, then flew to South Carolina. My old Jeep—unlike the idiot dogsitter's 1988 Mercury Grand Marquis—started right up, and we turned into the driveway twelve hours later. It seemed like we'd been home for two days, but even with the Slip-In visit it wasn't but four o'clock in the afternoon.

All of those numbers: I would not be happy the next day when the $100,000 Cash Five came out 11, 35, 2, 8, 12, I swear to God.

I replaced what once lived in the fireproof box and noticed how my social security card and an expired driver's license weren't in there. Back in the guest bedroom I picked up all of Josh's clothes, unmade the bed more so, searched between pillow and pillowcase, turned the duffel bag inside out, and had no personal identification cards flutter to the floor, which could have only meant that he had them on his person, as they said on those real-life police drama shows.

"Why did you keep an old drivers license locked up in the first place?" Vina asked.

I didn't tell her the truth: That I thought the mugshot made me look like Harry Dean Stanton in *Cool Hand Luke*, or *Paris, Texas*.

I left at dusk. Vina said we couldn't wait any longer. A poet-to-be probably engendered enough ridicule in or around the Unknown Branch of the Middle Saluda River during daylight hours, so nightfall could only lean toward bodily harm. I drove slowly in the direction that Josh took, and stayed on Old Hard Creek Mill Road for what ended up being 2.9 miles from my house. I took a left on Old Looper Rock Road and drove two miles, then U-turned, passed the mouth of Old Hard Creek, and went another two miles until the road dead-ended into an ex-logging road studded with deer stands. Understand that I kept both windows down and yelled, "Josh!" and "Poet!" and "'*The Road Not Taken*'!" about every fifty yards.

I backtracked and pulled my Jeep into every hunter's parking spot, left it running with the high beams on, and walked up and down trails until they disappeared.

I'd thought to bring along a phone this time and called Vina from the entrance to Carolina Rocks, a rock-dredging landscape outfit that I regarded as a front for something illegal, seeing as no trucks ever came in and out of the place. I ran into the owner Stet Looper only at Gus's Place, Laurinda's, or Miriam's—all roadside dives. But I guess I couldn't talk, either. To Vina I said, "Has Josh shown up yet?"

"I know this little trick," my wife said. "You probably found him two minutes down the road and y'all have been drinking this whole time down at one of your places."

I said, "Are you fucking kidding me? He's not there?" I looked at my watch. "I've been all over the place. And goddamn it, Vina, I'm not drinking. We got that pot, remember?" I said that last part quietly, seeing as there was no telling who might be hiding three trees back, listening, ready to follow me home, wrestle the baseball bat from my grip, and kill me over marijuana.

"His car's still in the driveway," Vina said. "Nothing's changed."

Before I hung up I asked her to check his back seat, just in case he returned, got confused, and passed out. I asked Vina to get out the dogsitter's keys and check the trunk.

As I got back to my Jeep, the door still open and the overhead light illuminating me in a way that I'd remember never to allow happen again, Stet Looper himself stumbled out of nowhere and blared out, "Can I help you with something?" He stood a foot or two out of the interior's light, and to the side of my headlights' peripheral reach. But I recognized his voice. Stet Looper'd gone to a number of colleges—or at least one college where he received a handful of separate degrees. Some people said that he postponed a return to running the family river rock business. Other people said that he was about a half-step away from leading a government overthrow once the economy finally imploded.

"Hey there, Stet. I'm looking for my dogsitter. We seem to have lost our dogsitter. First off we lost the dog, and now the dogsitter's gone missing. You haven't seen him, have you?"

"Murray? I thought y'all found Murray." Stet Looper walked around in front of the headlights. Was he wearing camouflage? Did he have his face tattooed? He opened the passenger seat and slid in beside me. "I thought I saw Melvina leading Murray out of the woods behind your house a few hours ago."

A couple hours later I would try to piece together why Stet wandered behind our house, or why he didn't call out to my wife. He had no reason to know my dog's name, for that matter. When I ventured out on my quarterly binges I did so alone, though I knew of people in the past who dogged up their cars while drunk, betting that highway patrolmen and sheriff's deputies would deduce that only a trip to the animal clinic took place. I said, "Yeah, Vina found him." And then I over-explained,

I realized, the entire chain of events. Sometimes I got nervous showing up at trailer doors back in the caseworker days and acted similarly. With Stet I began with the flight to Las Vegas and ended my diatribe where I sat, at the edge of his property.

Stet wore a special black-and-dark-green pants and shirt combo that I'd never seen hunters or soldiers wear. He'd covered his face in an intricate inky design usually associated with Maori tribesmen. "I haven't come across any strangers today," Stet said.

I pointed at his face. "You out hunting tonight?" No odor of booze drifted from his mouth or pores.

"People tend to disappear easily around here," he said. "My wife, for instance. She *said* she was going up to Minnesota in order to deliver our baby. She said that she didn't want any child of ours growing up around here and turning out like I did. Unless some things in the world of biology in general and gestation cycles in particular have changed without my knowing about it—like maybe how it takes eighteen months between conception and birth—then I'd have to say that she's gone missing in an intentional manner, too. Or maybe we live in an area prone to alien abductions. Or maybe this part of South Carolina urges us toward spontaneous combustion." Stet Looper smiled and shook his head. "Now I'm just being optimistic. They say that the guy who invented Microsoft Windows Vista is hiding out here somewhere, trying to escape lynching."

Stet tended to ramble from one topic to the next. I had heard the story of his wife more than a few times, from Stet personally, plus the mailman, an itinerate driveway sealer, the water meter reader, and Sharilyn at the Slip-In, who referred to Stet as "Dizzy." I said, "I'm sorry."

"I'll keep a look out, though," Stet said. "First off I have to find my wife. Then'll come your dogsitter. I have to keep priorities. Some people say 'I have to prioritize,' but I don't think it should be a verb. That'll be my next battle—the battle of language!" He opened his mouth wide and raised his eyebrows. I concentrated on my bladder. "First the wife, then the dogsitter," he said, and maybe I blinked or looked down at the gas gauge, but he no longer sat beside me. Stet Looper exited silently, left the door open, and slipped back into darkness.

Not that I ever excelled in foretelling the future—obviously, or I would've never gone to Las Vegas, or played wrong lottery numbers in an obsessive manner—but as I drove home, still yelling out for Josh, I understood that we'd never see our dogsitter again. We would track down his divorced parents, his graduate school advisor, and two of his friends. They would say that they'd not heard from him. They would hesitate, then admit, "You know, I guess I haven't heard from Josh in a while." I would paste some of those photographs up at the Slip-In, and the bars, with "Lost Dogsitter" and "Have You Seen This Dogsitter?" printed across the tops. His car would continue to erode in the driveway. His dirty clothes would take the place of our soaked towels in the closet.

I would read the obituaries constantly, waiting for my name to appear, seeing as Josh had my old driver's license. I would wait for some kind of stolen identity notice in the mail. I'd think, What are the odds of someone wanting to steal my life?

When I got home I kissed Vina on top of her head. I told her I needed to go back on the job market so we could afford a fence and security system. I wasn't sure if she grasped the urgency of my decision. My wife didn't ask what caused me to make a decision. She watched a Discovery Channel documentary concerning migration patterns with Murray on her lap. My wife ate a microwaved burrito, potato chips, and a hunk of Gouda cheese. She didn't make eye contact.

HOW ARE WE GOING TO LOSE THIS ONE?

Alex Mull says it doesn't matter if the phone book's expired. What would it matter? It's not like costume shops go in and out of business. Alex has a plan—first the costume shops, then the taxidermists. Taxidermists don't go out of business either. He doesn't have any facts on hand, but he imagines that most men who mount animals learned from their fathers, and so on. The bartender hands it over and says, "Costs a dollar to use the phone," because he's never seen Alex. In most cases the bartender only charges a quarter for strangers, but since Alex wears a suit— no one has ever worn a suit inside Doffers Paradise Lounge—it doesn't seem like too expensive a request.

Alex says, "I got my cellphone." He pats the inside of his coat pocket. He turns to the Yellow Pages and tries to think of other places besides costume shops and taxidermists.

Doffers Paradise Lounge is three streets over and down from where Poe Mill stood before it burned down from either arsonists or the homeless, like about every other ex-cotton mill not yet turned into condos in South Carolina. At one time every stool and booth filled with men and women off their shifts, pockets full of money, hair full of lint. Nowadays the place attracts only what few retirees remain in the mill village, or college kids out trying to gain some real-world experience beyond Starbucks, or daring men and women alike willing to ask the bartender if he knows where they can find some crack.

"Are you Doffer?" Alex asks. Then he says, "I guess I'll have a Bud," and points to a display of choices behind the bar. There are no light beers, only Budweiser, Pabst, and regular Miller, all in cans.

From where Alex sits, he can look at the mirror and see out the window behind him to a house where, a week earlier, a crudely tattooed black man not more than twenty years old adopted a medium-sized stray mutt from the humane society where Alex has worked for three years. Alex got out of college with his degree in sociology, went straight to graduate school for a master's in public relations, and—despite offers from advertising firms in Atlanta and Charlotte—settled down in Greenville. His parents tell him that he should've never taken an elective course in ethics and a seminar on Darwin. His parents tell him one person cannot make a difference when it comes to behavior, whether human or canine.

That's about the same thing his ex-fiancée Laurie said, and thus why she's getting married to another man tonight at seven o'clock. It's why Alex wears a suit, in case he gets the courage to show up at the wedding on the other side of town, unannounced and uninvited.

The bartender, who's wearing a work shirt with "Slick" above the left pocket, says, "Young man like you from not around here wouldn't know." He sets the beer can in front of Alex and says, "Two dollars."

"I live here," Alex says. "I'm from here. My name's Alex." He sticks out his hand.

Slick shakes it firmly. He says, "Doffer's a job. Not a spinner or weaver. Doffer." He doesn't offer up his name.

Alex looks through the Yellow Pages, places a finger on a costume shop's phone number, and pulls out his phone. When a woman answers he says, "Y'all got any bear suits?"

The door opens, and an older man steps in, leaning on a carved stick. He says, "Another day, another doldrum." Slick reaches into the cooler and extracts a PBR. The customer reaches into his pocket, pulls out four quarters, and stacks them beside the can. Slick slides them closer to his side of the counter.

Alex says, "Thank you anyway," and hangs up. He looks at the new man's stick and says, "Cool. Did you carve that yourself?"

The man sets in lengthwise on the counter. There are snakes and frogs carved into it mostly, but the handle's a dog's head. He says, "Yessir. That's about all I do now. Sell it to you for forty dollars."

Alex thinks, That would make a great wedding present. He says, "Let me think about it."

The man says, "Shupee."

Alex smiles. He thinks it might be some local way of saying, "Hurry up," or "I'll be here until you decide."

"I sign every one of them, right down at the bottom." He points. "Shupee. That's my name right there."

"Among other things," says Slick. He laughs and looks at Alex. "You just come back from a funeral? I hope you ain't *going* to one with beer on your breath. That ain't right."

Soon enough, Alex thinks, he will explain, in detail, the entire situation about Laurie. And he'll admit that the man she's marrying is some kind of national mountain bike champion named Todd, that they're going on their honeymoon to a number of trails so he can keep up his regimen, so Laurie will learn to love the sport as much as he, so they can—this is Alex's theory— use the entire honeymoon as a tax write-off. Alex figures he will even ask the bartender and Shupee what they think about his plan: to dress up in a bear suit and try to scare the new groom on one of the trails they're going to ride up in the Blue Ridge.

They'll think that they're talking some sense into him.

Alex checks the mirror. He sees the black man come out on his porch, the mutt beside him on a leash.

———

Alex hadn't considered the danger when he volunteered to track men who adopt probable pit-bull bait. He'd said to his boss, "If we can just get it in the breeders' heads that we're on to them, that'll slow things down somewhat. And we can also get some of them arrested."

His boss, rightly, said, "No."

But Alex made a decision. Until today, he hadn't realized that perhaps he profiled pit-bull breeders as young African American men with barely visible green tattoos on their biceps, and that more often than not he found himself following these men out into the country or back to the failing clapboard houses that surrounded mill villages. He took notes. Sometimes he came back at night and circled the prospective breeders' neighborhoods, looking for incriminating activity; in his mind he saw himself calling 911 while watching men, hundred-dollar bills waving above their heads, betting on dogfights in the front yard of one of these residences.

Laurie had warned him about this. She had said, "I bet if you got on the Internet and did some research, you'd find out that there are little old white women adopting pit bulls, or adopting stray dogs used in training pit bulls." Alex knew that she probably had a point. As a nod to her—even after she left him, met the guy who wore a helmet on his head more often than not just like some kind of shell-shock victim, and got engaged within a few months—Alex followed every tenth old white woman home. They all seemed to have whirligigs in their yards, he noticed. That had to mean something sociologically, he thought.

After three beers Alex looks at his watch and reminds himself to set a pace. Four hours until the wedding. The black man with the stray mutt has gone back inside his house.

Shupee says, "No. Whatever you do—and Slick will agree with me on this one—don't go dress up in a bear suit and try to scare your old girlfriend and her husband. First off, you'll get caught somehow. And when you get caught, you'll come across as—what's the right word here?"

Slick says, "Idiot. Insane. Pathetic."

"Those are right about on target," Shupee says. "No, you need to do the opposite of all that. I ain't talking the opposite of a bear costume. What would be the opposite of a bear costume?"

They all think for a moment, and then Alex says, "Salmon."

"I ain't asking you to consider going up to the mountains wearing a salmon costume, I'm asking that you act as though she don't matter none to you anymore. Do the opposite of pining. You don't want to appear that you pine for her." Shupee picks up his stick and looks at it. "This is from a tulip poplar. It ain't pine. Maybe you need to carry this stick around with you all the time as a way to remember."

Alex smiles. He shoves the telephone directory back to Slick. He says, "I think you're probably right. How much did you say that stick costs?"

"Sixty dollars."

"Let me keep thinking about it. I might go fifty."

Slick pulls out an *Iwanna* newspaper from under the bar. He says, "I might get me a pop-up camper. I made the mistake of promising a pop-up camper for the grandkids. I might get me one and just park it in the back."

Alex thinks of this as a perfect opportunity to say, "I read the other day where people are keeping their pit bulls in pop-up campers so as to make them meaner. Something about the confined space, you know, and they get meaner."

Alex tries to read their faces. Slick turns the page of his newspaper. Shupee says, "That sounds pretty dumb, but I wouldn't know." He looks at his wristwatch. "Daggum it. Today is Friday, right? I got to go get Francine's baby. I keep forgetting that I promised to get Francine's baby. Hold my spot," he says.

He takes his cane off the bar and leans it between his stool and the counter.

Alex waits until Shupee's gone. He says to Slick, "All that talk about pit bulls seems to have him a little antsy. Is it my imagination, or did he seem a little uncomfortable?"

Slick says, "What? No. Shupee just forgot about his wife's new boy. He keeps him on Fridays and Saturdays so Francine and her husband can have some alone time."

Alex nods. He thinks, You mean *grand*son. Who would keep his ex-wife's kid if it wasn't his?

He looks at the mirror behind Slick and notices the black man again, this time sitting without the dog. Alex turns around to look out the window. He says to Slick, "What's the story with that guy?"

Slick meanders around the bar counter and looks out the window. He goes to the door, opens it, and yells out, "Hey, Lawrence! Man in here wants to know your story."

Alex says, "Shhh. Shhh." He laughs. He reaches for Shupee's carved stick.

Lawrence waves and goes back inside his house. Alex turns around to Slick and says, "Don't do that, man." He points for another beer, then presses down on Shupee's cane to test its rigidity.

The door opens, and Shupee walks back in with a baby in a car-seat carrier. He sets the thing atop the counter and says to Slick, "Some things don't change. I got yelled at for being a half hour late."

It's a boy. He doesn't cry.

Alex points Shupee's stick back his way and says, "That's your son, or grandson?"

Slick says, "There he is. You can ask him yourself," as Lawrence walks into Doffers Paradise Lounge. He wears a sleeveless T-shirt, and his blue jeans ride low. Shupee says, "What's up, Lawrence?"

Lawrence says, "Hey," and turns his head around to look at Alex. "I know you. I got my dog from you,"

At first Alex thinks about denying it all, about saying something like, "I've never seen you in my life," or "I have an identical twin." He says, "You wouldn't have a bear suit by any chance, would you?"

"Are we back on that?" Shupee says. He takes a beer from Slick. "I thought we had that all settled before I left. Goddamn. I can't leave for five minutes. Loosen your tie, son."

Lawrence sits down between Shupee and Alex. He says, "I know you from the humane society. I saw you four or five days ago, man. You were right there."

Shupee asks Slick to turn on the television. He says, "The Braves are playing an afternoon game. I want to see how we're going to lose this one. They're playing the Cubs. I want to see how either one of them's going to lose."

Alex nods his head at Lawrence and says, "That's right. I'll be damned. You got that old mutt."

Lawrence stares at Alex, then looks to the bartender. He says, "Hey, Slick, I'll have a Miller's and a Goody's Powder." To Alex he says, "That ain't no mutt. That dog I got from you has some of that dog-jump-off-the-ship-when-the-Spanish-Ramada-sank-offshore in him. You know what I'm talking about? Wheaten terrier. Those dogs jumped off and swam to shore."

Alex thinks, I don't think *Ramada*'s the right word. He thinks, That dog you got is not whatever you're thinking. If anything, it's a wirehaired pointing griffon. He says, "I've had too much to drink." Then he imagines his ex-girlfriend and her new husband checking into a Ramada Inn somewhere outside of Barcelona, ready to take on any mountain bike trails of the far-off Pyrenees.

"He's thinking about going to his ex-wife's wedding," says Shupee.

"No, man!" says Lawrence. "Big mistake."

"She was just a girlfriend. She wasn't my ex-wife. Shupee's exaggerating. She wasn't my wife ever."

Slick opens up the *Iwanna* again. He says, "I'm thinking I might get me a tiller. I need me a good tiller."

Shupee's wife's son raises his hand and groans. Shupee looks up at the television set and says, "They'll find a way to lose, believe me. They should be called the Atlanta Confederates, or the Atlanta Rebels. No offense, Lawrence."

Lawrence says, "I got you, Shupe."

"I know you're thinking this got to be my grandboy, but it ain't," Shupee says to Alex. "Let's just say that my wife and I split up, and she got remarried, and then this come out. Who'd've known? It ain't like we didn't have a child. We got us two children, both went to college as a matter of fact. And then she got remarried and had another at age fifty-two. It's not some kind of record. I mean, it might be some kind of record here on the mill hill, but it ain't no kind of *world* record. I checked up on that. I thought I might could get us all some money for that."

Shupee shakes the bar of pickled eggs on the bar so that they swirl around like a poor man's lava lamp. His ex-wife's son turns his head slowly and smiles. He lets out another groan. Shupee nods.

Lawrence says, "How they going to lose today?" and jerks his head at the screen. "You got your error, your blown save, your walk-off home run. Who wants to make a bet? I say walk-off homer."

Alex stares at the child. He looks normal. He's not cross-eyed, overly obese, or missing fingers. Alex glances back up to Shupee and says, "That baby looks a lot like you."

Shupee keeps his eyes on the television set. He says, "Change the subject."

———

At six o'clock Alex loosens his tie. He's proud to have shut his mouth and listened since Lawrence came in. The dog that Lawrence retrieved from the humane society, as it ends up, will be a gift to Lawrence's grandmother, once the dog's house-trained. Finally, Alex says, "A wheaten terrier will never become house-trained, my friend. I mean, he won't pee or crap on the floor, but getting him to stop running in circles around the yard, or getting him to obey *sit* and *lie down* and *shut up*? Forget it. Those dogs are incorrigible. They're loveable as all get-out, but they're wild. Maybe that's why the Spanish Ramada sank. Maybe the captain was running around trying to catch his dog."

Lawrence says, "*Armada.* Yo. I hear that, my brother-man."

Shupee lifts his head up for Slick to pay attention. He mouths, "Coffee," for Alex, who is now slurring his speech. Shupee says, "One more hour and you won't have to worry about going to that funeral no more."

Lawrence looks up at the television and says, "This will be the answer. They're bringing in that guy from the bullpen. Anybody want to take some bets as to how many pitches before he gives up a home run?"

Alex orders another beer, but Slick acts as though he doesn't hear him. Alex says, "It's her wedding. Not a funeral, a wedding. And I have a confession to make." The left side of his face is an inch from the counter. He's eye level with the bottom of the baby carrier still set atop the bar. "When you said 'bet,' it reminded me."

Slick looks at Shupee and says, "That reminds *me.* Maybe that's why I said 'funeral.' I thought of something else you need to take with you in your coffin. A anvil. So's in case to go to heaven, somehow, and you don't like it. Maybe a anvil will bring you back down to earth, and then through it, and on down to hell."

Shupee laughs. He pulls a bent and smudged Mead memo book from his top pocket and flips through pages. He motions for Slick's pen, then writes down *anvil*. "I'm up to forty things.

Might have to hire on some extra pallbearers, especially with an anvil in there."

Lawrence says to Alex, "What kind of confession?"

Alex holds up his finger and says to Shupee, "What're y'all talking about? What're you taking in the casket?"

Lawrence says, "I know what that confession's all about. You followed me to where I lived just to make sure Simone was getting a good home. You people were thinking that a nice wheaten terrier deserves the best house possible."

Alex shakes his head. "Not even close. I thought you got the dog in order to kill it by pit bulls. It's a long story that may or may not involve ethnic profiling, and I'm not proud of it. As a matter of fact, I'm ashamed. It wasn't my idea," he says, lying. To Slick he says, "Can I get a beer for myself, and two for Lawrence? I have some payback. I owe him. I feel guilty as all get-out."

Slick looks at Shupee. Shupee nods and says, "I got his keys already. Let him do what he wants."

Alex feels in his pocket, notices that he doesn't have his keys, but doesn't ask how anyone got them. Lawrence says, "Thanks, man. No problem. My people have been putting up with such since the beginning. I'm used to it. God will set it straight to you white people one day. You folks need to learn what people are, and be what people learn."

Shupee turns to Alex and says, "I bet you never thought you'd come in here today and learn so many things, did you? People we get who ain't from around here, they come in thinking they'll be surrounded by the lost and the losing. But we're some regular philosophers, when it all boils down."

"Explain it," Slick says. "I'm not taking any credit for this one. Most days I think it's outright stupid, but you never know."

"See," Shupee says, picking up his cane—the baby cries out three times, widens his eyes, and expels a spit bubble that won't pop on his lips—"I don't want to say that I believe in an afterlife, but I'm afraid that if there is one, I won't be happy with what they got to offer. I sure know that things ain't exactly worked my way in this life. So. What I've come up with is this: I want to be buried with a crowbar, in case you *can* take it with you, and in case I want to pry myself out of a situation. At least that's how it all started. Then I realized that maybe I should be buried with a fire extinguisher—you know, in case I need to cool off the flames. Slick here just added the anvil. I've also got some them cold packs they got stay frozen up to seventy-two hours, my two pistols, a battery-operated Sawzall, one them blowup sex dolls, a bullhorn in case I go upwards and need to give some advice for the baby, and I'm hoping for a mostly-filled oxygen tank, in time. There are some other things. I keep forgetting to record them when they come to me." He flips through the pages.

Alex stares at Shupee for a moment, then says to Lawrence, "I'm all for restitution, if it matters any." Shupee shows everyone where he's carved an angel and a devil on both ends of his cane.

At seven Alex starts humming the Bridal Chorus from *Lohengrin*. Everyone has a pickled egg in his possession, even the baby. Slick had run one under tap water for a couple minutes to lessen its heat. Alex thinks, Would I ever be able to take care of Laurie and Todd's child if she asked me? He thinks, I need to remember some of those accouterments, and he wonders when was the last time he used the word *accouterments*.

He says, "Todd," elongating the name.

There's been a long rain delay in the baseball fame. The teams need to finish, since they won't meet again this season. TBS shows a rerun of *Gunsmoke* during the delay. "You need to quit singing that song," Slick says to Alex. To Shupee he says, "You need to change that baby before the crowd comes in."

Shupee says, "It's the pickled eggs that smells. It ain't this boy."

Alex says, "What crowd? Please tell me it's not karaoke night or something. Is it karaoke night? I hope it's karaoke night."

His cellphone begins to vibrate. He looks at the readout and sees that it's his old college roommate Paul Borick who, more than likely, is attending Laurie's wedding. Paul studied architecture, became an architect, and never questioned his decisions. Alex flips open the phone and presses the answer button. He says, "Where are you?"

Paul says nothing. Alex can just barely hear what must be the preacher asking Laurie and Todd to share their special, from-the-heart, spontaneous vows. Alex motions for Slick to turn down the volume to *Gunsmoke*. He looks at his new comrades and whispers, "On three, y'all yell out 'Don't do it!' like that. Loud as you can."

Alex figures Paul Borick must be sitting on the aisle, maybe only a couple of rows behind the bride's parents, holding the phone out and away from this body so Alex can hear this sacred moment—so, when Slick, Shupee, Lawrence, and Alex scream *"don't do it, don't do it, don't do it,"* over and over, both Laurie and Todd must turn from the altar. Shupee's stepson lets out a wail that may be even more audible than the drunken Doffers Paradise crew yelling. The guests must be craning their necks. Paul's phone clicks off.

Alex says, "Hello? Hello?" He smiles toward Lawrence and says, "Hello?"

Slick turns the volume up on the TV, and Festus says, "Well, I suspect there's a time and there's a place for such mischief, Matthew."

The baby settles down. Shupee says, "I can't believe that's what's on the TV right after what we done. Walkie-talkie! I been meaning to write down walkie-talkie for something in the coffin. Or half of one. Talkie."

They sit silent until they all seem uncomfortable. Lawrence says, "I need to feed Simone. She starts eating the table legs if she don't get her good on time."

"Bring her in here," Slick says. "I don't mind. Hell, she's got to be more hygienic than a baby crapping his pants."

Lawrence leaves. Shupee says, "He's a good man. Lawrence's a good man. I'd trust my life with Lawrence."

Slick says, "Uh-huh."

When *Gunsmoke* cuts off just as the bad guy's pulled his pistol on a little kid who spooked him, and when there's nothing but dead air for five seconds before the baseball game resumes, Alex thinks about how he could've made a mistake, easily, by turning Lawrence in for fighting dogs. He thinks about how he could be standing at a church altar with Laurie at this moment, confused from the sound of four invisible men screaming about how it's all a mistake. Alex thinks, I have a mission in life—I'm here to make sure that dogs and cats live better lives than dogs and cats.

He bends his beer can in the middle with his thumb and middle finger. With his fist he squashes it straight down into the size of a puck. Slick says, "There *might* be a crowd. One night there might be a crowd. If I don't keep thinking that, I might as well quit."

It's the seventh inning when the game resumes. Lawrence returns with his ex-stray on a makeshift bungee cord leash. Shupee puts his stepson down on the floor in his car seat. The dog licks the baby's face repeatedly. The baby waves his arms, then lets out a squeal. On the television, one of the announcers points out that no one has left the stadium during the long delay. The dog bounces up and down below the pickled egg jar, then lunges at Alex playfully, tongue lolling. Alex closes his eyes and wonders what it would feel like should Simone change her terrier mind. He imagines the dog tearing into his calf, jerking her head back and forth, digging deep into muscle.

He opens his eyes. Simone sits at attention, her paw atop the baby's leg. Shupee tries to get the child to hold the dog's leash.

After the pitcher warms up, rain begins to fall again. The camera turns to the stands where a man in a bear suit—perhaps a locally known unofficial mascot—holds his gigantic furry head in his hands. Alex starts laughing, points to the screen, and says, "That's not me. I could've been that guy, but I'm not."

The baby doesn't seem interested in the dog or the leash. Shupee pulls out another round of pickled eggs for everyone.

THE FIRST TO LOOK AWAY

OUR HOUSE'S VALUE, I understand now, never increased after my father completed the moat. My mother never warned him against such a project—at least not outwardly—but thinking back on this misguided venture it would be difficult to conceive of any excitement on her part. My father started off using the Increased Incidents of Documented Rabies argument, and ended with some kind of notion that, should he decide to sell off his river rock business and uproot to warmer climes, prospective buyers would clamor over a log house situated on its own island. Raccoons and foxes and feral pigs couldn't cross the canals, as long as we kept the two planned catwalks up, drawbridge-style. My father rationalized daily for a week that a real estate agent would have no problems convincing her clients that a house surrounded by water would be like living on the Love Boat.

"Or Alcatraz," my mother said, looking out to where the Unknown Branch of the Saluda River would detour into my father's manmade trench. She lit a cigarette each time she said this, took a couple drags, then stamped them out on a windowsill that she insisted was petrified wood anyway.

I didn't know how he understood to design it thusly without the use of a backhoe and level. I do know how embarrassed I felt when, out of nowhere, my fifth grade teacher announced, "Now, class, I want all of you to wear work clothes on Friday. I'm going to send a note home to your parents reminding them, and you'll need to bring either a shovel or a pick ax. We're going on a field trip to Stet's house, to dig for the rubies and sapphires! Why didn't you tell us you lived on a ruby and sapphire farm, Stet?"

I stared at Ms. Sebhatu, an Ethiopian woman who came to the United States as a teenager, rescued by missionaries (according to her). Then she was forced—I pieced together later—to attend a Baptist institution of higher learning where she discovered, evidently, that her old tribe's animist beliefs made more sense than the magic tricks scattered throughout the Bible. Looking back, I doubt Ms. Sebhatu could've ever been hired at a normal public school, but at Andrew Jackson Prep—which attracted students both black and white on both sides of the North and South Carolina border—she fit in perfectly with the prevailing embittered mentality of both students and their ancestors, though I supposed that Ms. Sebhatu owned some palpable and rational reasons.

This was on a Monday. Ms. Sebhatu would be talking about the field trip for another four days, I knew, just like when we got in a bus and drove all the way into Greenville in order to learn how wastewater got treated, followed by a trip to the coroner's office. The entire week before, she kept reminding us to bring gas masks or respirators or surgical masks, Mentholatum to put on our upper lips, and Pepto-Bismol.

I froze. My classmates stared at me. Justin Gardiner twirled a Frisbee on his fingers—the Andrew Jackson Fighting Jacks' Junior Varsity Frisbee Golf team was playing John C. Calhoun Prep, our arch-rivals, that afternoon—and said, "Your daddy pulls out regular old flat rocks from the river. He ain't got no safaris."

Ms. Sebahtu once said that she liked for him to keep a Frisbee at the ready, for it reminded her of the Surma women of southwest Ethiopia wearing lip plates back on the home continent.

I said to Justin, "Yeah he does." I thought, What if they ask me why I've never brought any of these precious gemstones into class for show-and-tell? I thought, What if they ask me how come my mother didn't wear spectacular shiny earrings when parents volunteered for PTA, or had bake sales to raise money for a new gym called "The Hermitage," or when she showed up for conferences because of my inability to contract A.D.D. like everyone else—my teachers said I concentrated *too* much. One time I stared at a math problem for three class periods trying to figure out the answer, because there ended up being a typo in the textbook.

Justin said, "How come you ain't ever brung any diamonds to show-and-tell?"

I looked at Ms. Sebahtu for some help. She smiled, wearing her special Monday turban that had smiley faces on the fabric. I said, "You're not paying attention to the grammar lessons, Frisbee boy." I said, "Why don't you bring in any bags of trash to show off, seeing as your dad's a garbage collector? Hey, why don't you bring in your sister on Explain Your Job Day so we can understand prostitution a little better?"

Sometimes my mother got called in for conferences because I had what the principal called "a smart mouth."

"Learning what hard work feels like is a valuable lesson," my father tried to explain to me when I got home and asked him about the field trip. "Y'all might learn that you want to do well in school so you don't have to dig ditches the rest of your lives."

I looked at my mother. She shook her head, rolled her eyes, dried her hands off on a dish towel and said, "If anybody needs me I'll be in the bathroom pouring Drano into the sink and toilet. Possibly my esophagus." Sometimes she accused my father of dumping river silt into our septic system just to keep her busy, to keep her from buying used high school annuals from across the South in hopes that she'd happen upon a famous or infamous person's photograph and then resell the yearbook. She said it was like a twenty-year bet, and that if she bought them for five dollars each and then sold them for over a hundred, it was better interest than what the banks offered. I hadn't learned how to compound interest on a five dollar bill over two decades yet, and always stared out the window for hours at a time when she spouted these difficult multiplication problems into the air.

I said, "Are there really rubies and sapphires on our land? Why didn't you tell me? How come you don't get some of the part-time workers to dig for them instead of pulling regular old flat rocks from the river?"

My father smiled. He said, "Well, there might be. There's only one way to find out, isn't there?"

I said, "This is a trick."

On his way out the door my father took me by the arm. "Come with me and give me some advice, Stet. I need to know what you think."

He didn't, of course. What he wanted me to do was join his insane one-man team in order to help convince my mother that his river redirection plan wasn't on par with most Army Corps of Engineers projects. As we walked down the slope toward the Unknown Branch of the Saluda River, then veered upriver, I said, "I sure would like a car."

"You ain't old enough yet," he said.

"A four-wheeler. An ATV. I could use an ATV. I could drag pallets of river rocks up toward the road. It might also keep me from telling Ms. Sebhatu that we have no emeralds or rubies or sapphires or diamonds. Gold."

My father patted my head about eight times, each tap increasingly harder. He said, "Stet, Stet, Stet, Stet. You know why I named you Stet, son?"

I said, "For a Stetson. That's what you told me before. You named me for a cowboy hat."

We continued walking until we came upon a stob my father'd driven into the soft river edge. He said, "No," and turned to admire the log house his father had built. "No, it's because 'stet' is a term used by editors when they realize they made a mistake.

Let's say an editor thinks a word is misspelled, and he spells it differently, then he gets out a dictionary and finds that *he* was wrong—not the writer—he writes 'stet' out in the margins. S-T-E-T. It's like saying, 'I thought I was right originally, but I made a mistake. My fault.'"

I said, "Why don't they just write, 'OK'"

"It stands for 'let it stand.' Kind of like you're standing here right now, today. With your father. Right?"

Normally I could follow my father's train of thought. Normally he said something like, "Get out the weedeater," and I knew that if I complained his next line would be, "Or *I* will, and I'll lash your legs with it while you're sleeping." One night he actually feigned doing this, but it ripped up the sheet down toward the foot of my bed and my mom dialed 9-1-1 until Dad convinced her that he was kidding, that me made a mistake in judgment.

I said, "Right. I'm with you. Standing."

"Stet. Or should I say, 'Let Him Stand'—your mother didn't want to have children. As you may have noticed, we only had one. I was all for having a child. She wasn't." Right away I knew two things: My father told a lie, and he shouldn't have been saying any of this. "So in a way, your being here is because of me. You have a good life, don't you, Stet? You're having a pretty good time overall, aren't you?"

I said, "Yes sir." It was the truth. I loved the river, and I got some kind of satisfaction from watching my parents argue in ways that were both nonaggressive and abnormal. I said, "I'm not thinking about suicide like most of the kids a year ahead of me. I'm happy."

"Good, Stet," he said. "Good, good, good. Then I guess you can see where this is going. You're a smart fellow. You can understand that if we don't make a moat around the house, then I'll be unhappy. And if I'm unhappy, then everyone around me will be unhappy, right? It's called cause and effect. Now we don't want any *effect* nosing around our business, do we?"

I shook my head. I had a feeling that my father kept a tape recorder hidden somewhere nearby, if not under his shirt. I said, "We can always fill it back in if it doesn't work out." Already I kind of imagined stagnant water and mosquito larvae.

"I believe I can handle one ATV, son. One ATV, on order." He touched his temple with his right index finger.

I said, "We might need a moat in case we really do find some rubies. Then everybody would be sneaking onto the property, wanting to dig."

My father said, "Huh. I never thought about that." He said, "Hot damn. Promise me this: If you think you find a ruby or sapphire, don't yell out anything. Just put it in your pocket."

I said, "OK."

Then we walked to an outbuilding and got out a four-wheel chalk dust contraption I'm pretty sure I'd seen at my school, out by the soccer field. My father made me push it in an arc around our house, outlining where my classmates would soon dig.

There was no way possible for my classmates to dig a proper moat, at least not in one Friday. It didn't take a surveyor to point out that our house stood at least ten feet higher than river altitude. I didn't need to stare off in the distance and calculate out that if we dug ten feet and an inch behind our house, then remained level to the water, the moat wouldn't be but an inch deep all the way around, not counting flood conditions.

I stood at the end of our driveway with a chamois cloth on a stick in order to wave the rarely-used field trip-driving bus driver down. There was no sense, my father said, for me to take the bus all the way to school, then return with my class, et cetera. Let me say now that I thought about hiding out in the woods, watching the bus go past our house, then returning to my father at around noon to say Ms. Sebhatu must've changed her mind. But I knew about both my parents' obsessive behavior, and how Dad would simply reschedule the event.

They showed up early. Right there seated over the wheel well was our principal, a driven woman named Dr. Futch whom we all called, of course, a number of things behind her back, and who always said, "Bad word!" when someone yelled out her name, seeing as it sounded such. I overheard my mother tell my father Dr. Futch's story one night—something about how she trained to play the viola but failed as a musician; then subsequently received advanced degrees in education but failed as a teacher; then became an administrator. Later on in life I recognized this continuum often, especially after three undergraduate degrees and part of a low-residency master's in Southern Culture Studies. Every time I got sent to Dr. Futch's office I noticed two paperbacks turned over open on her desk, but it took until college before I recognized the significance. One book was Machiavelli's *The Prince*, the other Chairman Mao's *Little Red Book*.

Sometimes our principal herded us into the cafeteria at Andrew Jackson Prep and gave us motivational speeches that stretched two or three class periods, and all ended with us having to chant "I will not ruin the community, I will obey" over and over.

"Welcome to Looper Mines!" my father yelled out, smiling, as my classmates descended.

Ms. Sebhatu walked a wide arc away from the river and came to shake my father's hand. She said, "Thank you so much for having us, Mr. Looper. This should be very educational."

"Hey there, Ms. Sebhatu," he said, pronouncing her name correctly for the first time. He'd practiced, I knew.

Dr. Futch lined everyone up single file and had them hold shovels across their shoulders like rifles. She said, in an eerily quiet manner, "'To link oneself with the masses, one must act in accordance with the needs and wishes of the masses. All work done for the masses must start from their needs and not from the desire of any individual, however well-intentioned.'" Straight out of Chairman Mao, I learned some dozen years later while taking a course in college called The Variety of Communist Experiences. The professor had that Andy Warhol print of Chairman Mao on an easel of sorts, the mouth cut out, and he liked to stand directly behind it and offer up aphorisms in what could best be described as a politically incorrect Chinese dialect. I don't know if it was the power of suggestion or what, but I left that class every Monday-Wednesday-Friday and went down to order egg rolls for lunch more often than not.

My classmates grabbed their shovels, and I grabbed mine, and my father directed everyone to the apex of his property and pointed out where to dig. Ms. Sebhatu said, "So where is the flume line? Where are the screens?"

My father looked at her a good five seconds. Later on he would say to my mother, "How the hell does a woman from Ethiopia know so much about mining for sapphires and rubies? Are there ruby mines in Ethiopia that I've somehow missed reading about? Why don't those people in Ethiopia just sell off all their giant rubies and sapphires to the jewelers of the world and use the money to buy food that's at least a step up from a bag of free flour?"

A girl from my class named May-May wandered down by the river. Ms. Sebhatu called out to her, "Do not let your shadow fall across the river water, May-May. If a fish or turtle bites your shadow, there goes your soul." She turned back to my father, awaiting his answer.

May-May drug her shovel behind her and said, "When's lunch? I'm hungry. My parents told me that my diamond earrings are more important than any of these nasty rubies."

My father said to Ms. Sebhatu, "It's called dry mining." To the class he announced, "Remember the three Cs—color, clarity, and crystals. Rubies and sapphires always have a crystal formation with six sides. And you're looking for a kind of dusky red color for the rubies and about any color between black and white for the sapphires."

I looked at him. He made eye contact for about a tenth of a second and looked away. Where did he find all of this knowledge on gemstones? On the porch of our house, my mother held a coffee cup to her mouth and shook her head. May-May sprinted up the steps, banging the shovel. She said that her parents let her drink coffee whenever she wanted it.

Each of my classmates—and me, too—held up every single stone we uncovered and said, "Is this a ruby? Is this a ruby? Is this a ruby?" because they were all somewhat red from the clay.

Dr. Futch pulled some pom-poms out of her bag—her *real* dream in life finally come true—and cheered us on throughout the entire ordeal. Maybe there were similar words in one of the Ethiopian dialects that Ms. Sebhatu grew up speaking, but it sounded like she said "Oy vey" every time Dr. Futch tried to perform a toe touch, right front hurdler, spread eagle, or left herkie jump. I kept my eyes on the ground and dug.

We didn't uncover any gemstones, or if we did there was no one around to identify them correctly. We uncovered some nice chunks of quartz, and a couple of my father's buried childhood dogs. Ms. Sebahtu ran back to the bus and wouldn't come out when Justin levered out a small homemade pine coffin, brushed off the front, and read out loud, "Here Lies Rex—1953-1962." He turned to the principal and said, "Can we open it up and look inside?"

My father yelled out, "Rex!" and began weeping immediately. He took two or three steps toward the coffin, then looked at the sky in much the same way I did when concentrating to the point of catatonia.

I said, "That wouldn't be good luck, I don't think. Maybe we better put that thing back in the ground." Three feet later we uncovered a dog named Moses, which I remembered my father talking about because it would barrel across the river in such a way as to part the water.

May-May—who hadn't dug one shovelful yet and said that her parents sent a note explaining how she couldn't ever perform manual labor because it might affect her piano fingers or her debutante-to-be calves—said, "I've had six poodles, but when they died we had them cremated and placed in urns." Later on in life I understood that if I'd've taken my shovel and gotten a good swing at May-May's head, the world would be a better place.

The rest of my classmates and I, though, dug until we had blisters the size of bubble wrap. My mother finally came out on the porch and put a stop to it all. I'm not sure if she wanted to protect my father, but she came out and yelled, "I don't know why y'all are wasting your time. It's not even sapphire or ruby season! It's not the right time to dig. Everybody get on up here for some homemade pie and ice cream and ginger ale. And vitamin E."

Dr. Futch held her pom-poms up in the air above her head, then brought them down to a T formation. She chanted, "Push 'em back, push 'em back, w-a-a-a-a-y back," maybe, I guess, thinking that we had to refill the ditch. She shuffle-footed in reverse. Even only being fifth graders, as a group we turned and witnessed the beginning of our principal's long downhill struggle with dementia. Ms. Sebhatu yelled through one of the open windows of the bus, "Were you trained to play the viola or the kazoo?"

My father dropped his shovel and stretched his back. He said quietly to no one in particular, "This is a good start. I can get some day laborers to finish it off."

My mother provided Band-Aids, Bactine, Neosporin, ice packs, sunburn lotion, and a threat to May-May if she talked any more about her wealthy parents and the fountain that they had in their front yard. Ms. Sebhatu finally eased back out of the school bus, but she looked to be in shock, and she mumbled something that I took to be her religion's special protection prayer against disturbing the dead.

At two-thirty my classmates boarded the bus and went off to what I imagined would be a weekend filled with muscle aches. They took with them all the chunks of quartz that we found and piled off to the side, for the principal decided that it might be educational to have a rock garden of sorts somewhere between the science room and the cafeteria. As one final shot toward my mother, May-May yelled from the bus window, "My momma's got diamonds bigger than these quartzes."

In the house my father said, "Y'all did some good work out there today, Stet. I guess we know now that indeed we don't live atop a gem mine."

For the first time I remember, I stared at him until he was the first to look away. I said, "How long did it take you to bury those dogs? They were pretty deep. If you knew then what you know now, maybe you should've just continued digging until you had a moat."

My father began crying again, got up, walked down to the river, waded in halfway, and just stood there. Me, I got the telephone book and looked up backhoe and trencher rental information. Then I went back out with my shovel to dig harder and deeper than anyone.

It took us two months. When my father had an excess of river rocks loaded up on pallets and no landscapers in the offing, he paid his one full-time employee Mr. Welling to shovel out what ended up being a twelve-foot wide canal that ran in a beautiful Bell curve around the house, except for two stutters to avoid Rex and Moses' graves. I worked after school most days, and saved the quartz to add to Dr. Futch's collection. She later made all of her teachers and staff attend a motivational speech performed by an honest-to-God motivational speaker, and they heated up those rocks in a bonfire, spread them out, and walked across the hot coals in some kind of ritual that supposedly manufactured instant feelings of teamwork and community. I remember all of this because our school got shut down for a week when I was in sixth grade because there weren't enough substitute teachers available while the regular ones sat at home with their legs elevated, nursing third-degree burns on their soles.

Anyway, we dug the moat about fifteen feet at its deepest, hit a spring that helped us out, and finished off the task with my father at the moat's entrance and me at the exit. On the count of three we dug like crazy the last couple feet toward the Unknown Branch of the Saluda River. The water entered, and by the time it rounded the house I had clearance for it to meet back up with where it belonged, on its way to the Congaree, and then to the Cooper, and finally somewhere into the Atlantic outside of Charleston. At least that's what my father told me and how I envisioned it—not counting lakes and dams in between.

My father then dropped timbers across, and built a couple walkways. Sometimes I sat on the planks and dropped a line in, hoping that trout took refuge in our manmade diversion. They didn't. Sometimes I rode an inner tube around the house. It got old fast.

"Tell your father that he needs to account for erosion," Ms. Sebhatu said on that first Monday back after the field trip. She stood at the entranceway to the room, as if wanting to catch me alone. A few members of the class didn't show up, and their parents called both the school and my father. "Once that water begins digging into the soil constantly, over and over, the island will shrink." Did my father tell her of his scheme? Were all ex-Baptist animists mind readers?

I said, "Yes ma'am."

"Perhaps that is how South America and Africa became separated," she said. "Maybe someone had a grand idea of digging a ditch the length of what is now Brazil and Angola, among other countries' coastlines. Perhaps. Perhaps the water finally floated them off from each other into two giant islands. You wouldn't want that now, would you?"

Ms. Sebhatu wore her smiley face turban. She didn't smile, though. She didn't blink. Her countenance held a wisdom carried down over millennia, as if the knowledge gathered from every generation now amassed behind her eyes. I said, "I wouldn't like that very much. If anything, I want to live somewhere else."

"That's my boy," Ms. Sebhatu said. She nodded. "Tell your father that he was right in his thinking: We all now know that we don't want to be unpaid laborers or slaves for the entirety of our lives. We have learned that much. You tell him Ms. Sebhatu relayed this information to you, Stet. And you, too, must learn from your father's bad decisions."

I thought, I'm going to fail the fifth grade. I said, "I might've been adopted."

We would refill the moat a year later. Sure enough, the Unknown Branch of the Saluda River flooded most of November and December, which caused the banks to flow away until the water chipped and exposed Rex and Moses until their coffins floated down to the mouth of the moat and lodged there. My father never really got over that sight. It changed him. We didn't pry the lids off or anything, but I supposed that only fur and bone remained inside. I helped him fish the pine boxes out and set them up by one of the outbuildings. Alone, he rigged my ATV with the back bumper of an old truck and shoved mounds of clay back into our fancy ditch. Then we reburied the dogs.

One day after sixth grade geography class I walked over to Ms. Sebhatu's room in the other wing of our school. I told her the story. She said we need not worry about rabid animals nearing our front porch, or even Jehovah's Witnesses. Ms. Sebhatu said she'd offered a special prayer for my fearful family, one that always worked, no matter which continent.

A MAN WITH MY NUMBER

THE MAN INSISTED THAT I needed stick-on numbers. He carried a special case that looked like a shrunken steamer trunk, with one handle and three large metal clasps. By "large" I mean the length and width of a playing card. I didn't check the thickness of each clasp. Most clasps aren't any bigger than the ones on old lunch boxes, or maybe briefcases. These were big clasps. I became enamored with them, and thought about buckles on the shoes of Puritans. I remember thinking to myself, This guy should be out selling *clasps*, not stick-on numbers. Clasps like that—hell, you could keep roofs from flying off during tornado or hurricane season with some clasps like that.

The man himself looked normal enough, if standing five-four and being thin enough to crawl into ductwork without grunting is normal. I was glad that I noticed this feature of him later. Also, it looked as if he combed his hair after a careful diagnosis from a slide rule, T-square, and micrometer. He had the eyes of a tent revival preacher, part blank and part bloodshot. I said, "Say that all again, man."

This was at the front door. No one ever came to my front door. Hardly anyone ever came to the side door either, except for the mail lady when one of my machetes, oversized boots, or special bolt cutters finally arrived. Or the UPS guy. Or someone with a stray dog saying it showed up at their house and everyone says it's probably mine—which it never has been seeing as I keep my dogs under control. If I had some kind of running-off dog,

I could use one of the stick-on numbers guy's trunk clasps to reinforce the dog's collar and chain.

But my dogs never feel the need to roam. People who know me—people who don't show up unannounced with a stray wondering if it's one of mine—know that my dogs somehow understand boundaries. They show up at my house for a reason, then settle in. Dogs seem to sense things we cannot fathom. They know fear, sure, that's all been documented. But they also know what kinds of people won't feed or pet them if they (the dogs) run out into the road or chase birds on a whim. Dogs know good music when they hear it, too.

The man said, "I notice you don't have any street address numbers out there on your mailbox, or anywhere on the side of your house. So it's your lucky day. I'm here to show you some stick-on numbers that won't rust, peel, bleed, fade, or become compromised by the elements. You ever seen that number ten over there in London, where the prime minister lives? They've been showing that entrance with the number ten now since Winston Churchill. Those are our numbers."

I said, "The nursery's closed. I'm out of plants right now. But I'll have some cypresses in the next few weeks." I had kind of presupposed, I suppose, what the man came for. When it wasn't dogs or lost people or the mail lady, it was people confusing my one-man nursery across the street with my private abode. I said, "Wait. I have numbers on my mailbox and right there on the side entrance so in case there's a substitute mail lady or UPS driver they'll know that they're at the right place to bring my machetes, oversized boots, or bolt cutters."

From the front door, you can't see the side of my house. It's around the corner. There's a jut. "I hate to contradict you, Mr. ...." This guy was good. This guy had something else going for him besides the mesmerizing buckles. He had a clipboard that he could hold in such a way that I couldn't tell if he really had any names written down, in up-and-down-the-road order, standing for the people who lived on Snipes Road.

I said, "Beaumont." It was the fake name I used when I needed to use fake names when people showed up. People always felt non-threatened, at first, around anyone named Beaumont. It was the last name of the actor who played Mr. Ward Cleaver.

The stick-on number guy said, "Here it is. Beaumont."

So I was *on* to him. Ha! To me he wasn't much of an authority on the stick-on numbers game anymore. I kind of wish I hadn't mentioned the things I collected, should he be one to collect the exact same things and want to come back and break in. I said, "Or when the mail lady or UPS driver brings me one of my many assault rifles and booby traps bought from down in South America." I looked way out at the mailbox. I faced it directly, so couldn't see if the numbers might be missing. I said, "What's your name, man."

He placed his clipboard down atop the trunk. He reached in his shirt pocket and produced an ID that can be bought at about any flea market worth its while. I had about twenty of the things I carried around with me at various times when I went out. He said, "Mack Morris Murray. Three Ms. That's one of the reasons I always knew I'd be perfect for this job. 3M, like the company that makes the best adhesives going around. People call me Mack Morris."

First off, I thought, Who would come up with a fake name like Mack Morris Murray? Me, my fake IDs weren't all that different than John Smith, John Jones, Joe Smith, Joe Jones, Mike Smith, Mike Jones. People like to make the acquaintance of people with easy fake names. People don't like other people with either A) a bunch of names that're all first names like "Mack" and "Morris" and "Murray," or B) a bunch of names that're all last names like "Pinckney" and "Calhoun" and "Sanders." Dogs don't like people with those kinds of names, either. Go introduce your dog to someone named Mack Morris Murray or Pinckney

Calhoun Sanders and see what happens. Growling dog, that's what happens.

I closed the door behind me, not thinking. Looking back on it all, that's another reason not to trust people with three first or last names in a row. They get a person too distracted.

I walked out into my front yard, which was four narrow acres, on a slant until I noticed that, sure enough, someone had stolen the numbers off of my mailbox. There's a place where I can look through the pine trees, winter or summer.

I walked around the jut of the house, stood on the gravel driveway, and learned that the same thing had happened to my house numbers. In my mind, walking back to this fancy-clasped salesman, I remembered what my numbers looked like in both places. I foresaw his opening the trunk, my seeing my numbers that he'd stolen some time in the past couple days, and then my going inside to get one of the machetes.

I said, "I don't have a lot of patience, Mr. Morris."

"Murray. Mack Morris Murray. Please call me Mack Morris," he said. "I don't know if it's the law around here, but in some towns it's the law to have visible and easily identifiable house numbers. For the fire department, you know."

I said, "Uh-huh. Well, 'Mr. Beaumont' might sound like a real nice guy, but he isn't always. You can ask his sons, wife, or that kid Eddie Haskell."

I kept eye contact. So did Mack Morris Murray. And he smiled one of those smiles everyone's seen. In Australia, smiles are frowns and frowns are smiles. I figured this Mack Morris Murray man to be Australian. He could disguise his frown just by living north of the equator. Mack Morris said, "I'm not so sure I follow you. Maybe it would be best I come back at another time."

A couple of my dogs barked inside. There were more in the back, behind the Leyland cypresses I planted myself, which hid the stone wall I built myself, which hid the cedar plank privacy fence I built with the help of a man named Guillermo some years earlier when the dogs started showing up.

I said, "No, you stay right here. Why don't you open up that fancy trunk of yours and let's you and me take a close inspection of what kinds of numbers you got for sale. I got a long address number, you know. It's nineteen, thirty three, seventeen. It's one, nine, three, three, one, seven."

Mack Morris said, "I got you. It's a hundred ninety three, three hundred seventeen."

"It's one hundred ninety three thousand, three hundred seventeen," I said as fast as possible. I'd practiced it before. Sometimes I like to give out my telephone number like that, too.

He said, "We don't offer any discounts on big numbers, if that's what you're asking. I can sell you one number at a time, though, if you're hurting for money right now. I can come back every month and sell you a number." He unclasped his trunk, right there on the brick walkway I also built myself. "They're two dollars apiece."

Mack Morris Murray opened the case full, and leaned the top of his trunk against the side of my house jut. Sure enough, there were about six different styles of numbers in there—the best ones were tile, the worst thin metal numbers cut on an angle. I didn't see any of my own, though. I said, "You got these numbers over at Monkey Grass Estates, didn't you. I know these numbers. All the big houses over at Monkey Grass Estates have these kinds of numbers, on their special stone mailbox holders, and on the exterior of the stone houses."

I used to live way out in the country. Within about a ten year period a bunch of children and grandchildren of farmers inherited their family land, then sold it off without conscience. Land developers took that opportunity to either A) build subdivisions made up entirely of houses that weren't under 5,000 square feet, or B) plop down house trailers that had been repossessed. There were no zoning laws, is what I'm saying.

And evidently there had never been any kind of special course the land developers could take on How to Name a Subdivision. The rich places on down Snipes Road had names like Monkey Grass Estates, The Rookery, and Neck of the Woods Acres. The trailer parks had signs leaning out on the road advertising Camelot, Belle Meade, and Vista Bella. It never made sense to me. Snipes Road ran a long way, too, unfortunately. You'd think the goddamn land developers would hurry up and make me an offer for the land where my nursery stands. Hell, those old boys could sink a good sixty or thousand trailers down on the two acres I own across Snipes.

He closed the lid to his trunk. Mack Morris said, "I guess I could get you a two-for-one deal. Or a six for three deal. That would come out a dollar apiece."

In his eyes I could see that he wanted to take off running. Where was his car? I wondered. I said, "How did you get here? Where did you come from?" I started laughing. "You walk down the road in one direction at night, stealing people's numbers, then come on back through in the opposite direction, trying to sell them back."

"I'll just give you some numbers," Mack Morris said. He reopened his trunk.

Listen, I've never had anything against scam artists and practical jokers. Me? I'm the man behind going out at night in boots four sizes too big, with a machete and bolt cutters—and sometimes spray paint—changing signs so they read Monkey Ass Estates. Neck Acres. The Nookery.

I said, "Are you a drinking man, Mr. Mack Morris Murray? Let's you and me go inside and partake of some schnapps I got holed up for a special occasion. I like your style, man. Or some brandy."

"I'd like just a plain old can of beer, to be honest."

"I got beer," I said.

Then I turned around to learn that I'd locked myself out of the house. I rang my own doorbell and both Now and Later showed up wagging their tails and barking at the long pane of glass beside my front door. One thing about non-running, boundary-knowing dogs, you can't teach them how to unlock a door. They can be kind of lazy.

"Is the side door open?" Mack Morris asked me. I shook my head. I held my finger up for Mack Morris to wait right there, and I jogged out on the gravel driveway, checked the knob, then jogged back.

I said, "I think the back door's closed, too, but there's a window I got that's unlocked. Thing is, I got one of my bolt cutters lodged in such a way that the window won't open but about ten inches. Let me give you a leg-up over the stone fence and the cedar fence, you go back there, lift the window, shimmy in, and come to the front door and unlock it."

Mack Morris said, "That's not the first time you've mentioned bolt cutters. Why do you have so many bolt cutters?"

We walked toward the side yard and wove through the Leyland cypresses that now touched each other side-by-side and stood twenty feet high. I said, "Cut bolts, what else?" I didn't say how sometimes I used them on my dogs' toenails.

When I got the number stealer balanced right so he could see my back yard, he said, "I ain't going over this thing. How many dogs you got, man? Those things will tear me apart."

I pushed him over. I'm no strong man, but like I said, Mack Morris Murray couldn't have weighed two big bags of cheap dry chow. My outside dogs barked, but they ran off to the far corner of the property, scrambling through a variety of potted azaleas, Leylands, boxwoods, wisterias, crabapples, and whatnot that weren't quite ready for me to take over to the nursery. I had a three-month rule when it came to people's—or at least land developers'—memories as to what plants got sold to them, stolen, then sold again. I'd like to say that these particular dogs were good judges of character, or that I trained them such, but to be honest they were mostly pussies. Mack Morris Murray called over to me, "Goddamn you. You better have two cans of beer in there."

Then I thought, What if he gets inside my house and starts stealing things? I thought, I'm an idiot—a man who steals numbers off of mailboxes isn't exactly trustworthy roaming around inside someone's house. I looked through the cracks in the fence and said, "Hey. Hey, wait a minute."

He said, "I found it. This window here? I found it," and I heard the window go up a little. Then I heard him slide right in, and close the window behind himself.

So I ran around to the front of the house, grabbed his trunk of numbers, touched the giant clasps all three, and thought about how at least I had this thing for ransom until he came out. I figured that if he found my machetes and came out the front door swinging, I could block some of the blows with the trunk.

But he opened the door presently. Now and Later stood there beside him, practically smiling, wagging their tails. I set down the trunk, and went inside. I said, "Thanks, man."

"You got to buy some numbers after all that. That's only fair," he said, stepping aside.

I said, "Uh-huh," and walked the long way around toward the refrigerator, inspecting everything to make sure nothing had been slipped into Mack Morris Murray's pockets.

Mack Morris sat down at the kitchen table. I pulled out four cans of beer and set them on the table. I reached into the cupboard and pulled out half a bottle of peppermint schnapps and half a bottle of peach schnapps. Mack Morris looked around the kitchen and said, "I can tell that your wife left you. Mine, too. That's why I'm doing what I'm doing, trying to get by. Yours take you for everything, too? Maybe they're together, living it up."

I tried to imagine the wife of such a small, slight, perfect-haired house number salesman. I said, "It's been a while. I still don't talk about it much." I didn't say, "Especially to strangers." To be honest, I'd only talked to the dogs about it, and most of them were either too young to remember my wife, or they hadn't been thrown out of moving cars yet, abandoned.

Mack Morris opened a can of beer. He scooted back his chair, leaned back, and extended his short legs. "I'll tell you my story if you tell me yours. First off, my wife—let's call her Barb, seeing that's her name—Barb was a churchgoer. Hell, so was I. We went to church. You can't condemn a man for going to church and believing that the Ten Commandments are a good thing. Or the Golden Rule."

I unscrewed the plastic top from a bottle of Mr. Boston Schnapps. I didn't even look down to see if it was the peppermint or peach. Sometimes I did this. Well, every day I did this. It was my little game. I looked up on the wall at two machetes displayed, and wondered how long it would take me to get up, grab one, and take a hundred and eighty degree swing at full force. Answer: two seconds. I'd timed myself often, over the last few years, when all the dogs were out back and out of harm's way. I needed to know how fast I could cut off one of Mack Morris Murray's arm should he stick it out with a Bible attached, wanting to pray for me, this house number selling only a ploy to offer testimonials to the unsuspecting. I said, "OK."

"Let me make it clear that it was a regular church. It was Methodist. Then out of nowhere Barb started thinking that everyone concerned about the Greenhouse Effect was some kind of Satanist. She thought they had some kind of made-up agenda in order to make money. Why would a bunch of scientists make up such stuff about glaciers disappearing? There were pictures and videos of it! Why would they go to the trouble of faking videos of ice melting on both ends of the planet, that's what I ask you. And what I asked her."

I called Now, but not Later. I said, "Come here, Now." He did. He sat down by my side and stared at me. I could tell by the look in his eyes that he wanted me to put on some blues music. Now liked blues. Later liked Miles Davis and Miles Davis only. Some dog psychologist could explain it all, I'm sure.

"So Barb decided that God meant for everything to be. She took the notion of no free will to extreme measures. She said, 'All actions are Good. It's how God wants us to be. "Good" and "God" are close together in spelling for a reason. If He wants me to drive around throwing Styrofoam containers out my car window, then it's because He invented Man, who invented Styrofoam, and we can do with it what we will. God invented the Earth six-thousand years ago, and He did so understanding that we would go through cycles in climate.' I tell you what, when she said it to me, Mr. Beaumont, it was if a zombie spoke. She had a blank look. Her voice came out not unlike what a hand-turned sausage grinder sounds like with, I don't know, maybe *paperclips* shoved down the funnel."

I opened and drank from the beer. There was no way I was going to tell my story. And at this point I didn't trust Mack Morris Murray yet. I never promised to tell my story, even though he volunteered his. I said, "It makes you wonder." I had no clue what else to say.

"It makes you wonder, it does!" Mack Morris Murray said. He threw back his head and laughed in a way that I couldn't tell if it was fake or not. I know this: He opened his mouth wide, and I noticed for the first time that he had a large black spot on his tongue. He had a spotted tongue in the same way that a half-Chow, half-Lab does. At first I thought maybe he suffered from tongue cancer, and that he sold house numbers in order to pay for radiation, or chemo, or amputation. He reached for the peppermint schnapps.

I pulled back the bottle. I said, "You shouldn't be drinking this stuff. I think it might've gone bad. You shouldn't be drinking it." I felt bad, but I didn't want a tongue cancer victim putting his lips to my bottle. Or a possible mixed-breed devil.

"No, I shouldn't. I have a bunch of people to meet this afternoon," he said. He looked up at the two machetes, then turned around and looked into the den where another dozen were displayed on the walls. "They say a crow can tell if a man's armed with a pistol or not. They say a snake knows if someone walking nearby has a machete in his possession. What's the fascination with machetes, Mr. Beaumont? You afraid of snakes?"

I said, "My name's not really Beaumont. I made up that name."

Mack Morris Murray showed that godawful spotted tongue again. I'll give him this, though—his tongue wasn't forked, at least not physically. He said, "Your name's Leonard Scott, but people call you Pinetop. Somebody told me. That guy in the house down the road told me. Don't worry, it happens all the time. I should write one of those baby name books using only the fake names I've come across in this line of work." He reached for the schnapps again, and I let him take it.

I said, "They call me Pinetop? What does that mean?"

Mack Morris Murray pushed the bottle back my way. "It's not a secret, from what your neighbor said. You go out at night and destroy, or at least maim, the trees in the new developments. Then you go back later and try to sell them clippings from your Leyland cypresses, seeing as they can be grown from sprigs, or clippings, or whatever you call them. I steal numbers, you steal the lives of trees. So what? My wife would think that what you do is God's plan. Me, she'd think it was God's plan only if He invented numbers and wanted us all to abuse the things."

I said, "Come here, Later."

Mack Morris Murray said, "I used to have a regular job as a teacher. I know you probably won't believe half of what I tell you, but I used to be a teacher. This wasn't that long ago. I taught math. Hell, I even worked as a scorer for one of those national education testing services, you know."

I said, "Your tongue looks like my dog Later's tongue. Are you all right, or did you just chew up some licorice before you came over here? What's that stuff—did you chew some clove gum before you came over here?" I said, "I thought all those tests were scored by a computer."

"I did one of the other tests. I scored one of those tests that matter more. I scored one of the tests that gives out partial points even if the final answer turns out wrong." Mack Morris Murray closed his mouth hard. He stared down at both Now and Later. The dogs didn't seem to want to growl at him, like I thought they would, which could've only meant that the guy didn't really have three first names. Mack Morris Murray nodded his head a couple times, almost imperceptibly. He said, "I've always wanted to own a nursery, though. Nurseries kind of run like math. You have two plants, you have four plants, you have sixteen plants. I'm talking about hybrids now. Like your Leyland cypresses."

I said, "I wonder what your ex-wife thinks about hybrid cars. Why would God let Man invent a hybrid car if we were all meant to use up gas and oil and throw Styrofoam and used tires out the car windows."

"I never finished my story," Mack Morris said. "I got sidetracked. It's not your fault—I get sidetracked more and more these days. You're right. All that stuff about all that stuff. Yeah. So Barb took all the money we had in the bank and moved off to one of those places, and gave it all to one of those preachers. At least that's what I've gathered."

I said, "My wife's name was Audrey. It's not the same story. My wife left me because she said I was too ..."

My dogs started barking all at once. I got up and went to the side door to look out and see if someone else had showed up, maybe to sell me gutters he'd stolen off the house while Mack Morris and I talked at the kitchen table. No one stood outside, though. There was no car. I walked around to the front door and only saw the mini-trunk with the beautiful clasps. I opened the door, made sure it was unlocked, went outside, and retrieved the box of numbers. I brought them inside—a mini-trunk of numbers weighs more than you'd think—and was going to set it down on the kitchen floor, but I came in to find Mack Morris Murray holding my two kitchen machetes in each hand.

"You were too what?"

"Trusting," I said. I said, "Put those back on the wall, please." I'd never timed myself dropping a mini-trunk of numbers in the kitchen, running into the den, and wielding two of those machetes off the wall. The only reason why I kept so many machetes, I understood, was to prove to Audrey that I wasn't too trusting, and so on, should she ever return.

Mack Morris Murray said, "I'm just messing with you. I could've cut your head off twice if I wanted to, but I'm not that kind of man. Like I said, Gold Rule. Barb would probably cut off your head and say with a straight face that God meant for her to do it, you know."

I still held the trunk. Mack Morris Murray put one machete back on the wall, ran his thumb down the blade of the other, then placed it below the first. I said, "Goddamn you. I have to go pee." I went outside and looked through the kitchen window to keep tabs on his movements. He placed his head on the table, forehead and nose straight down. Back inside I said, "So that's my story. She said I let people take advantage of me. She said I sold plants too cheap, or believed people when they said they would come back on Friday to pay me in full. Then she left. Last I heard Audrey worked for a tax filing outfit. Last I heard, she dressed up like either the Statue of Liberty or Uncle Sam and tried to flag down taxpayers driving down the road between January first and April fifteenth."

"It's all about inventory. It's all about inventory with women. Well, no, maybe not women. With your ex-wife and my ex-wife. Speaking of which." Mack Morris Murray opened his second can of beer. He took his trunk of numbers from me and set it on the table. I unscrewed the peach schnapps and took two slugs. Mack Morris said, "I have to do this. It'll mean good things will happen to me later." He pulled out two ceramic 1s, two 3s, a 9, and a 7. He lined them up to read 193317. "Here," he said.

Then he took all the other numbers out and asked me to help him divide them up into style, and number. We stacked them up. He had a lot of ones, as it ended up, which made sense seeing as every street block needs ones. We went on down the line. He had more ceramic numbers than metal, more metal than plastic. When we finished I said, "That's kind of weird that you only have three sixes."

He stuck out his tongue and showed me that black spot.

I pulled out my wallet, dug out twelve dollars, and handed it over. I would've given him a tip, but I realized that I'd need to drive over to the closest hardware store and buy six or eight new bolt locks for my doors. Mack Morris Murray said, "Between you and me, it's a despicable world out there." He pointed with his chin. He refilled his mini-trunk haphazardly.

I said, "It can only get better," which I didn't quite believe, but tried to.

"Nice doing business with you, Mr. Beaumont. Or Leonard. Or Mr. Scott," Mack Morris Murray said. "Or Pinetop. You ain't no different than I am. Don't go around thinking that you're any different."

And then he left. I checked the door so it wouldn't lock behind me, and watched as he clomped through the middle of my front yard, appearing to know where I'd dug holes and covered them with pinestraw and switches. He took all the right veers, and high-stepped in exact places. At Snipes Road he looked both ways, then took a right-hand turn toward the residential developments. Because it's the country, and because sound travels, I could make out his whistling from afar. Was it "Onward Christian Soldier"? Was it "Amazing Grace"? Was it that song I didn't know the name of that everyone heard when a bride walked down the church aisle?

Back inside, I opened the silverware drawer. My wife's wedding band and engagement ring were gone. They no longer rested where Audrey placed them before she left, each placed inside silver napkin holders we had never used.

PERFECT ATTENDANCE

MADISON KENT'S FATHER SAID that they could eat anywhere, but Madison remembered this trick. The last time they saw each other—a month before the boy began high school—Charlie Kent offered the same boastful invitation. His son chose the Peddler Steakhouse, one of the pricier restaurants in town. Charlie Kent swung by a McDonald's on the way, and they ended up eating dollar-menu burgers and fries in the parking lot of the Peddler. So on this next occasion—the late afternoon of his high school graduation—Madison said, "I don't care" over the phone. "You pick. Maybe we can park beneath a tree."

Like the last time they spoke over the telephone, Madison heard traffic in the background—car horns, plaintive cries from people living in a neighborhood Madison couldn't picture. His father plunged change into a pay phone. Who used pay phones anymore? Madison wondered. Where were pay phones in the first place? Madison's only experience with a pay phone occurred back when his parents still lived together. They had abandoned a trip to Florida after the car blew an oil gasket and threw a rod. Charlie Kent sold the car for junk after two days of staying at a Motel 6 in Valdosta that had a swimming pool in back and a bar across the street. Madison's mother had walked across the street to get her husband, stopped at a pay phone mounted to the building's exterior, and called her sister collect. Later on, Madison's mother said she had to make decisions about her husband *and* her blood relatives.

"You think it'll be all right for me to be in the same audience as your momma? I don't want to get all settled down in my chair for your graduation and have your mother pull out a tape measure and decide I'm within however many feet I'm supposed to keep between us."

Madison said, "Are you still living in Myrtle Beach? Mom said for me not to expect you to really show up, especially if a bike rally is going on down there." Madison didn't say, "She said you'll just go off on a binge and forget," though she had. He wanted only for his biological father to forget Madison's given name.

"Living in Myrtle Beach, yes. Got me a job as a caretaker for a trailer park between South Myrtle and Murrell's Inlet. I'm a glorified handyman. They give me a place to live free. And a golf cart to go from one problem to the next."

Madison didn't know that his father could fix anything. His mother told stories of having to tie her ex-husband's shoes. Before everything fell apart financially, physically, and in the porous bubble of matrimony, Charlie Kent had worked as an H&R Block tax preparer, which meant that he kept busy from January until mid-April. He told friends and strangers alike, "For four months out of the year I work on numbers. For eight months out of the year, numbers work on me." Then he'd extract a joint from his pocket, sock, wallet, or from behind his ear, as if to prove that he never exaggerated.

His son couldn't think of a proper segue. He said, "Are you going to drive all the way up here, then turn around?"

Charlie said, "I've already heard from your mother. She says you changed your name. She didn't say if you did it legal-wise or not, but that you changed it."

Madison said, "Yeah, you never know about Mom. Maybe you shouldn't come to the actual graduation ceremony. First off, you're right—she might have that restraining order still going on about not being within a hundred yards of her. On top of that,

I'm just walking across the stage with four hundred other losers. I'm not the valedictorian."

"You like seafood?" Charlie Kent asked. "I eat nothing but the freshest seafood down here every day. Flounder. Scallops. Catfish. Crawdads. I know this sounds weird, but I miss fish that *ain't* so fresh. Y'all still got that Cap'n Del Kell's up there? Cap'n Del Kell's Galley Bell, is that what it's called?"

"Yes sir." He didn't bring up how catfish and crayfish weren't seafood.

"Let's you and me meet there. Your graduation's at two, so let's meet about four. That should be enough time, don't you think? Hey, you got a girlfriend? You can bring her along."

Charlie Kent's son *did* have a girlfriend, Laney. They would both be attending Reed College in the fall—either nine or eleven states away from South Carolina, depending on the route taken—on full scholarships. Laney, in fact, would be giving the valedictory speech. Her boyfriend, Madison, third in his class, would receive special recognition for never missing a day of school, from kindergarten onward. He would get booed, laughed at, and taunted by his classmates, and he didn't want his father to witness such a spectacle, especially after driving 250 miles.

"I didn't change my name. I just don't go by Chip anymore," Madison said to his father. A computerized voice asked Charlie to put in ninety-five cents more. "I'm using my middle name."

"You don't go by Chip anymore?" his father bellowed. "Damn, son. That was our whole thing—Charles and Chip. Charles Chip. Like those potato chips that come in a big can. Home delivery and everything. Your middle name? That's your momma's maiden name, right?"

"I don't think those potato chips come that way anymore," Madison said. "Yeah, we can't go around doing that anymore. I'm not even sure I've seen any Charles Chips lately."

"They still make them," his father said.

Madison thought, Maybe they're available at all fine pay phones everywhere. He said, "I go by Madison. It's not a big deal."

"Madison sounds like a lawyer's name. Or a fancy hotel," his father said. Then the line went dead.

After the ceremony, Madison drove to Cap'n Del Kell's Galley Bell alone. He left his friends—all of whom would come running back home one day after their college degree, he felt sure—at the entrance to the gymnasium, and said that he'd meet them later in the Wal-Mart Superstore parking lot. One of last year's graduates now ran a cash register, and promised to fake-check fake IDs. Madison kissed Laney, said, "Great speech," and left to see his father. His mother came up to him in the parking lot and said, "Call me when you order, call me when you're done. Do not let him talk you into lending him your graduation money."

In the history of seafood restaurants, Cap'n Del Kell's fell somewhere between Long John Silver's and Red Lobster. Cap'n Del strode around asking how everything was, and sometimes he drank too much and tried to wear a wooden leg. The waitresses wore bandannas on their heads, said "matey" more often than needed, and always approached a table with "What can we hook you up with?" They prided themselves on hush puppies.

Madison Kent said "lemonade" when the woman asked what she could "hook him up with." He thought at first, You can hook me up with a grammar textbook, and I'll show you how come you're not supposed to end questions with prepositions, but he decided against it. Laney might've done so, seeing as she graduated first in the class.

"I'm waiting for someone," Madison said. He looked at his wristwatch. "Maybe I'm late, though. Has anyone come in here saying he was waiting for a Chip?"

The waitress pointed at her name tag, which was the shape of a curled smiling shrimp. She said, "I remember you. You graduate today? I'm from last year. I'm just doing this until I get into dental hygiene over at Tri-County Tech. I ain't doing this the rest of my life. Like I see it, though, I get to take notes on people's teeth while they chewing, you know. I ain't got all the technical terminology down right, but from what I can see firsthand, most people dining at Cap'n Del Kell's either got gum disease or a variety of problems with their canines, all the way through their molars. Anyway," she said, still pointing at the flat plastic shrimp below her collarbone, "I'm Karla."

Madison thought, I remember her being a cheerleader. He said, "Yeah, Karla. I know you."

"I'll bring the lemonade. You going to be waiting long? I'll bring over some fish nuts while you're waiting."

Madison didn't have time to ask what they were. He yelled out, "OK," but Karla had gone in the kitchen.

"Hey there, Chip," his father said from behind Madison's booth. "I know the back of a Kent head from a mile away."

Madison didn't know whether to say, "Hey" or "Hey, Dad," or "Hey, Mr. Kent." He giggled nervously, and blurted out, "Our waitress used to be a cheerleader." Charles Kent sat down across from his son. His broad, pink face beamed. Madison hadn't seen his father in four years; he remembered less hair and more Vitalis or Brylcreem.

"Does this place serve beer?" his father asked. "I don't drink anymore. I mean, I don't drink *every day* like the old days, but I'll have a beer or two on special occasions. You know what I mean? You and me—let's have a beer, and order some fried oysters."

He looks like that actor who's always having a mug shot aired on TV, Madison thought. He said, "I have to be twenty-one."

"Screw that, son. Are you kidding me? They don't teach law in high school anymore?" Charlie Kent said, his voice high. He rubbed both his sunburned arms down toward the tabletop, and his son couldn't tell if sand or dead skin landed. "You with a parent, you can drink all you want. Hey, cheerleader. We need some service over here."

Madison almost said, "Dad." He said, "Come on, she'll be here. Shhh."

"Can I help you?" Karla asked. She held a squirt bottle of tartar sauce in one hand and her order pad in the other. "Y'all ready?"

Charlie Kent said, "I'm Charles. This is my boy Chip. Charles, Chip. Charles Chip."

She said, "Uh-huh."

Madison said, "She already knows me as Madison. Back in high school I went by Madison."

Charlie Kent lifted his scaly eyebrows. He said, "OK. Not a problem. I bet you were scared how I'd react, taking your momma's maiden name and all. Fuck. Madison's better than another million names. It's a president's name, by God. It's a president's name, and it's better than Adams, or Jefferson, or Roosevelt for a first name."

Madison remembered his mother's stories: His father swore off drinking one time, but within a week came back from the grocery store loaded down with three dozen jars of Vita brand pickled herring in wine sauce. The next morning Madison's mother found the jars sucked dry, the fillets standing on edge in their containers. She told a story of his father one time scraping his knuckles on purpose so he could apply isopropyl to the abrasions, in order to lick the alcohol. Madison could remember others.

Karla said, "I know you ain't twenty-one."

Charlie Kent said, "Damn. A psychic! We can't get past her. Maybe you should get a job down at the carnival." He tousled his own hair, making it stand up in unnatural ways. "What do you want, son."

"Lemonade."

"He ordered lemonade already," Karla said.

"Y'all got any vodka? Y'all ain't got no vodka, I know," Charlie said, craning his neck around in search of a proper bar. "OK. One lemonade, and let me get two beers so you don't have to keep returning to us every five minutes. Two draft beers. I don't care what y'all even have, as long as they're not light. Y'all got regular, regular draft on tap? I want two of those. And his lemonade."

Madison looked at his father. Karla didn't question Charlie's order. She returned with beer, lemonade, and straws. She said, "Your teeth are in good shape."

Cap'n Del Kell kept a cheap gold-plated bell by the door, with a sign beside it that read "If All Went Well, Ring Cap'n Del Kell's Bell." Various knotted ropes hung on the walls. The booth backs had been painted to resemble the sterns of Key West and Cape Cod yachts. Charlie Kent raised his mug. "Perfect attendance, huh? Damn. I'm proud of you, son. I don't think I ever went a month without missing a day of school. Back then, though, I had to help out on your granddad's farm."

Madison didn't process this last statement. He didn't mention how his father's father sold insurance, lived in a subdivision, and never seemed to dress in anything outside of a short-sleeved white shirt and slacks bought from the back page of a Sunday magazine. Madison said, "How'd you know about that? Were you at graduation?"

"Saw it on the news. It was on CNN, a big thing on how only a few kids nationwide never missed a day of school." Charlie drank half of his beer. He said, "Beer tastes about the same here as down in Myrtle Beach."

Madison sat forward. "Are you kidding me? Did you record it? We don't have cable TV anymore. I didn't see it."

Charlie Kent smiled. He rose his hand to Karla. When she approached he said, "We're both going to get the fried shrimp and oyster extravaganza. Y'all use real mayonnaise in your cole slaw?"

She said, "Fried shrimp's my favorite."

"If the cole slaw's made with no-fat mayo, or whatever it's called, you can keep it. And listen. I know this'll sound strange. But Chip and I have this old family tradition where we eat our shrimps and oysters using fancy toothpicks. You know what I'm talking about? You got any of those toothpicks back there with the cellophane twirled on the other side of the business end?"

Karla said, "A toothpick can be a valuable tool in the prevention of gum disease and tooth decay." She said, "We use them on the BLTs. I'll bring you a handful."

"I don't remember that particular tradition," Madison said. He remembered his mother locking his father out of the house when he showed up drunk at two in the morning. He remembered his father, drunk, throwing his own socks, underwear, and ties into the fireplace on Christmas morning, and his father borrowing the neighbor's dog whenever he drove to the liquor store drunk, for he believed that no police officer would arrest a drunk man driving his dog around town. Although Madison tried to block certain memories, he saw himself leaving the house for school and hearing plates crashing into walls behind him—that particular tradition.

"You weren't on CNN, Chip. I mean, you weren't on CNN, Madison. Goddamn. Are you sure you're ready for college? Maybe you should've played hooky a time or two and watched some kind of documentary on how gullible people can't make it in the real world."

Madison's cellphone vibrated in his pocket, then rang. He said, "I bet it's Mom."

"I bet it is, too. You better talk to her. Settle her nerves. Let her know that I didn't kidnap you back to having some fun."

Madison flipped open his phone after his mother had hung up already. He said, "Hello?" and paused. "That's so nice. Thank you, Mr. President."

"The *president's* calling you?" Charlie Kent said.

Madison shoved his phone back in his pocket. He shook his head, smiled, and pulled the other mug of beer his way. "I think that makes us even. Dad."

Karla said she piled three or four extra shrimp on each platter. "My graduation present to you," she said to Madison. "What did you get him, Dad?" she asked.

"I haven't given it to him yet," Charlie Kent said. "I still got it in the car." Karla dropped a couple dozen toothpicks down on their folded paper napkins, then left for a table of two other graduates that Madison knew, with their parents. "I meant to wrap it up, but I was running late," Charlie said to Madison.

"You don't have to give me anything," Madison said. He pushed his father's beer back across the table. "That stuff's nasty. I don't like beer."

Charlie Kent took the paper sleeve off of one straw. He looked around, then sat up to check on Karla's whereabouts. "Watch this," he said. He stuck a fancy, frilled blue cellophane toothpick in the mouth end of his straw, leaned his head back, and blew hard. The toothpick stuck in a textured ceiling tile above their booth. "You ever done anything like that?"

Madison said, "Please don't do that. We'll get kicked out of here."

"It's like horseshoes. It's like that bowling game the French people play all the time. In a perfect world toothpicks are blue, red, and yellow. Or green. Now, you blow one and see how close you can come to that first one. The first one's like a stake." Charlie Kent picked through the remaining toothpicks and said, "I'll continue being blue. You're red. We'll just remember the original stake up there."

"No." Madison ate one fried shrimp and set the tail down on the side of his plate.

"You might go off to that fancy college in Oregon and end up studying anthropology and need to know how indigenous people shoot blow guns," Charlie Kent said in a singsong voice.

Madison envisioned shooting a toothpick across the booth perfectly and landing it in his father's forehead, or eyeball. He said, "I'm serious. How'd you know about that award I got?"

Karla brought two more mugs of beer. Madison wondered if he'd missed his father making some kind of secret sign, or if Cap'n Del Kell instructed his waitresses to keep them coming no matter what. Karla said, "Everything OK?" She didn't look up.

"Great!" Charlie Kent said. "You're the best." He smiled in an unnaturally large way, Madison thought, then said, "No."

"Eat up," Karla said.

Someone rang the bell, and exited.

"No matter what she says, your mother still loves me," Charlie said. "I ain't bragging. And I know that I wasn't exactly husband material. I'm a good father. I could *be* a good father, if your mother would let me. Please understand that when I talk to your momma—and I do way more often than you'd know—I always ask that she let you come down and live with me. I've got a fold-out couch, after all. And we have a high school you could've gotten to without missing a day."

Madison tore the end from his straw and blew the wrapper toward his father. It dive-bombed into tartar sauce. "I'm not going to study anthropology," he said. "I don't know what I'll end up doing, but I'd bet that I'm going to major in mathematics, or astronomy. I would also be willing to bet that Mom told you that, too."

Charlie Kent blew two toothpicks at once. One veered off like a haywire missile and stuck in the ceiling three feet from the original one. The other actually hit the first toothpick and fell back down onto their table. He said, "So tell me about this young woman Laney. Would I approve of her?"

When he daydreamed about the future, Madison saw Laney and him graduating from college, then going off to graduate school, then joining the Peace Corps. He saw himself trying to convince tribe members that they could count beyond, "One, two, many." Madison said, "She's really smart."

"That don't cut it," Charlie Kent said. "Smart cuts it only in France. Does she have a nice set? Does she give it up?" He picked up a homestyle fry and shook it at his son.

"Laney's perfect," Madison said. "Don't worry about it."

"Your mother was perfect," Charlie said. "I bet you can't shoot a toothpick and land it anywhere between those two up there."

Madison said, "Some people now call me Mad. Or Madman." He stuck a red-ended toothpick into his straw and blew it hard at his biological father. It, too, landed in the tartar sauce.

"You're a terrible shot," his father said. "Listen. I want you to do something for me. I want you to talk to your mother. I *know* she still has a little fire in her for me. She never got remarried, did she? Did she ever even date anyone? You know, and this is neither here or there, but I didn't have to help her out once you turned eighteen. I kept on sending in child support, though. I sent in what I could send in. I've been working kind of part-time, doing people's taxes at the trailer park, you know. I use that money to help you."

"I don't care what y'all do after I go to college. Y'all can get remarried for all I care." Madison picked the breading off of his oysters and set it aside. Laney's mother had had a gallbladder attack twice.

"I don't think that's going to happen," Charlie said. "Maybe we could live together, at best. I could quit all my bad habits for ten years and your mother would find a way to bring them up once a day. Person like her drives people into drinking and doing drugs. If you're going to be guilty all the time in someone's eyes, you might as well have fun."

Karla came up to the table, took a French fry off Madison's plate, and ate half of it. She said through clenched teeth, "I'm looking the other way best I can. Hurry up with that beer before Cap'n Del shows up. He always shows up around six." She placed the other half of her fry on top of Madison's discarded breading, and skipped to another table.

"She likes you, Chip," Charlie said. "She's flirting with you. Hotdamn to be young again."

"No she's not. She's a cheerleader. Cheerleaders don't go for guys who make straight As, except in American history." But Madison wasn't thinking about what he said. No, he thought of Laney, and how she brought up daily how he couldn't get his grade point average up to second in the class. *Every day* she found ways to bring up, "I'm first and he's only third" into the conversation. They could never watch a baseball game together, Madison knew, or she'd bring it up every half inning.

Charlie Kent reached over and picked up an oyster from his boy's plate. He said, "Anyway, your mom and I aren't getting back together. The company that owns my trailer park's starting up another development way up in some place called Pleasant Unity, Pennsylvania. I might be asked to move up there and get things started. I might do it. That's one thing. I also have this buddy who's a bagrunner, needs some help."

Madison said, "Running drugs?" He reached over and drank more of his father's beer. It wasn't as bad as the first had been.

"No. Idiot. Driving lost luggage out to hotels and such." Charlie Kent laughed. "What's your mother been saying about me? I don't do drugs anymore. Too expensive, for one. Anyway, my buddy's a bagrunner, and he says that the airline industry— especially Delta/Northwest—is so fucked up that you might as well forget seeing your suitcase arrive when you do. I ain't even talking about making a connection in Atlanta or Charlotte. I'm talking you get on a plane for New York nonstop, and they send your Samsonite to Nova Scotia. Luggage could write a travel book, man."

Madison blew a toothpick into the ceiling. He and his father tried to high-five each other and knocked over a full mug of beer.

"I guess I'm supposed to give you some fatherly advice," Charlie Kent said. "One, don't take any wooden nickels. Two, don't ever work for H&R Block, and probably not for Delta or Northwest airlines. Three, make sure your wife has a sense of humor, and some patience. Well, don't ever get married and you can strike off that little problem right away. Four—do you have a checking account?—write a bad check so you don't go around worrying about having bad credit all the time." He drank from his mug. "Five. Goddamn. I practiced this whole speech on the way up there. I had six things."

Madison said, "I don't care if you call me Chip." He craned over to the beer with his straw and sipped hard. "You can call me Chip."

Karla brought two more mugs. She said, "Cap'n Del called in sick. Do you know what this means? He never calls in sick. They say he ain't missed a day since his wife died two or three years ago."

"Thanks, Karla," Madison said. "I tell you what, when you become a dental hygienist I'm going to start going to a dentist every month. You know what would be cool? If you could clean teeth, and do a split at the same time."

"Five!" Charlie Kent yelled out. To Karla he said, "Well, we're sorry that we're going to miss Cap'n Del. Give him our regards." He gathered empty mugs and slid them toward the table's edge. Turning back to his son Charlie said, "Five. Your first day of college? Miss all your classes. Listen. Every day you show up for school, or a job, or a marriage—it's like winding up the rubber band on one of those balsa wood airplanes with the plastic propeller. Sooner or later the rubber's going to crack up and break, you know what I mean?"

Madison looked at his wristwatch. He thought, I need to call Mom. He said, "I have to pee," and got up. In the men's room, which had only a toilet, he locked the door. He punched his home number, it rang four times, and the answering machine picked up. He said, "I'm still here. Everything's fine. Dad might get a part-time job as a bagrunner, which isn't the same thing as a drug runner, according to him. Anyway. I'm still here. Cap'n Del called in sick, though."

He hung up, then peed in the sink.

When Madison returned to the booth, he found his father sitting there with his plate pushed aside. In front of Charlie Kent sat a folded map of the southeastern United States, an auto parts calendar, and a car jack. "Happy graduation," he said. "Like I said, I'm sorry that I didn't have time to wrap them up. Six—I remembered the sixth piece of advice—always have a dog with you, no matter what. And get a stray. Don't go buying some kind of fancy pedigree. I meant to get you a dog for your graduation, but I figured it'd be best if you picked one out yourself. Plus it might be frowned upon by your roommate."

Madison sat down. He said, "Dad."

"Anyway, these are all things you might need in the future. Fold-up map? You need to find a way back home, correct-o? The jack's so you can either change a tire, or mess with your roommate's bed in college. One day I'll tell you what I did to my roommate in college. The story takes too long. It involves a foldout from one of those magazines, a bunk bed, and his girlfriend. Your mother knows all about it. She was there! Your mother knows all about it, but she wouldn't want me telling it yet. The calendar's so you'll know, you know, the date. So you'll know that it might be the day not to be such a goddamn drone. Worker bee. Ant, you know?"

Madison thought to say, "So I'll be totally irresponsible, like you?" but didn't. He thought to say, "Go put this shit back in your car," but didn't. From what stock do I hail? he thought. He said, "Thank you."

"There you go," his father said. Charlie Kent pushed against the table, but it didn't move. "So," he said, "what did your mother get you?"

Madison's mother had saved her spare change from his birth onward, and put the money in a savings account. She'd handed over a certified check for ten thousand-plus dollars. Madison said, "A microwave oven."

Charlie Kent blew another toothpick into the ceiling tile. Madison looked up and noticed that he'd blown others while Madison was absent from the table. Charlie said, "That's practical. That's good."

Karla placed the bill down. She said, "I ain't rushing y'all none." A man rang the bell and walked out. She yelled, "Thanks, Mr. Looper." Back to Madison and Charlie she said, "He might be crazy. They say his wife took off for somewhere, and he might be crazy."

"Well," Charlie said. "Huh."

When Madison pulled out money from his wallet, Charlie Kent didn't stop him. Madison understood that, in the future, he'd be paying his father's bills, more than likely. He envisioned his being a professor somewhere, teaching freshmen and sophomores the importance of pi, or how come some rocks in southern Utah exist only there and on Mars, and then meeting up with his biological father at a fast food restaurant, in South Carolina, or Pennsylvania, or the Pacific Northwest. He imagined Charlie Kent waving his right hand, saying he didn't need help. Madison foresaw his being there always, should his father need help.

Madison didn't have a wife in any of these scenarios.

"You got something to do?" Charlie asked.

"I'm supposed to meet some friends at a party," Madison said.

Charlie looked out the plate-glass windows of Cap'n Del Kell's Galley Bell. He said, "It's almost dark." He pointed outside and said how he would have clear weather on his drive back. He said that he needed to get back home so he could look at someone's trailer axle. Charlie said, "You know what? Let me borrow that jack of yours, and the map, too. I'll bring it back next time. I'd hate to have trouble going home."

Madison said, "I agree."

"You keep the calendar, though. I can get back home fine without a calendar." Then he pointed to the array of toothpicks stuck to the ceiling and said, "Look, the Big Dipper. It's always there, somehow. Every time I do this, the Big Dipper always comes out."

On his way out of the restaurant, Madison asked Karla if they needed any help. He said he wanted only a summer job, nothing permanent. She told him to come back the next day at six o'clock to meet the captain, and be on time. She told him to lie, though, and say he planned on working there forever.

WHERE STRANGERS CLAIM THE TARNISHED

BILLY CRUME'S FATHER "INVENTED" the Hole in the Head safety device, and that's what brought me, desperate, into He's Out Casting. I kind of remembered my mother shoving a Hole in the Head-type rig to the top of my ears before scrubbing my scalp down with Ivory soap back when I sat in bathtubs. Then, for some reason, my mixed breed dog Gypsy—this was before ethnically-sensitive people correctly named dogs Roma or Hashkalija, or even Irish Traveler—sported the Hole in the Head for a month or thereabouts. She might've had ear mites. Maybe my chore was, among other things, to shove drops down Gypsy's ear canals, and keep her from clawing at them, which a Hole in the Head would do automatically. I can't recall exactly. We weren't a family who took pictures of our pets, even when they wore awkward don't-get-shampoo-in-your-child's-eyes plastic collars. Someone should undergo a psychological study as to why some 1970s families found it necessary to keep a camera at the ready in every room of the house, while others didn't. This was a time before those wacky TV shows embarrassing everyone. If you ask me, human beings who didn't go down to the Eckerd's or Kmart to get film developed every goddamn minute of the day should be given Good Citizenship certificates from the Sierra Club and the EPA for not helping pollute streams with whatever chemicals get dumped out after the entire photo development process. Sure, the psychological community might concur rightly after proctoring a bombardment of MMPIs that a family without pictures of their pets and/or children might lean toward antisocial, if not downright pathological, but at least they're not groundwater-tainters and eco-terrorists.

Anyway, Crume evidently inherited a mini-storage warehouse full of Holes in the Head, and when I called him about this stock that he'd advertised in the want ads he asked that we meet in a bar. Billy Crume intimated over the phone that he couldn't let anyone know the location of his merchandise, or his own street address, and so on. I told him that I understood, though I didn't, then.

I don't want to make any presumptions about paranoia, but Billy Crume's father and mother, I believed, didn't take too many photographs of his growing up, either.

Crume got there before I did and sat at the very end of a short wooden bar where eight people could sidle up facing the bartender and two to the front door. This was on the Laurens County side of Lake Greenwood in a town called Waterloo. Since I'd been brought up in South Carolina and had heard of Waterloo all of my life—there was a well-attended yearly Kill the Gar Festival here that attracted fishermen of sorts from far away as Georgia—I didn't think of the town, or my meeting Billy Crume, in any sort of historic/ironic context. I just packed up my tape recorder, memo pad, two pens, and roadmap, then told my wife Abby, "I'm heading for Waterloo to talk to an old boy about his daddy's failed invention." I didn't need to explain how I had a paper due for Dr. Theron Crowther as part of my low-residency master's program in Southern Culture Studies down at Ole Miss-Taylor. And I didn't add, "I think this might be a real story," seeing as every time I had done so in the past, the paper never worked out.

Abby said, "I'll be working on my speesh impediment all day long," for she still had hopes of one day getting a job as an anchorwoman, somehow. She might've said how she wanted to go out and look at some things for our upcoming baby, too.

Right as the door closed from our house she said something like, "bashinet," and "shafety sheat."

I said, "OK. Be careful," like I always do.

It wasn't difficult to choose Billy Crume in the He's Out Casting lineup of imbibers: He wore one of the Hole in the Head safety devices. In case this isn't quite clear yet, here's what his father invented—a Frisbee with the center cut out. A caring, yet reckless mother placed the thing over her child's head before shampooing so that suds didn't get in the kid's eyes. The Hole in the Head was an opaque plastic, and although I didn't bring along a micrometer I would say that it ranged in the ninety-thousandths of an inch range, which isn't as thin as it sounds. Later on, after I gained Crume's trust, he let me hold it in my hand, where I could read "Tupper Seal 224-2" on the rim. It also read, "U. S. Pat 2487400 Can Pat 463387 Other Pats Pend." Crume told me that this particular Hole in the Head was from Tupperware's Millionaire line, which had been printed in the center of the burp top before his father either cut or burned it out for fitting's sake.

I walked past a row of four men who emitted a variety of odors that started with floating-fish-on-stagnant-water and ended with nightcrawler-guts-on-hands. The walls facing the bartender—I didn't bring in a tape measure, either, but this lakeside joint wasn't much more than thirty by sixteen feet—held what appeared to be the shellacked snouts of gar. Counting those scary prehistoric mandibles, the place wasn't but fourteen-and-a-half feet wide. There was no net covering the ceiling, but there were red-and-white plastic bobbers glued to the plywood. After a dozen bourbon and Cokes one might think he sat lake-bottom looking up at the surface.

"I take it you're either Billy Crume, or he's talked you into buying one of his hats," I said. "I'm the guy who called last night. Stet Looper."

Crume didn't wear stained khakis like his cohorts. He didn't wear a fishing cap beneath his Hole in the Head, with lures hanging from the brim. Billy Crume didn't wear a T-shirt that announced "I'd Rather Be Fishing," or "My Other Shirt's a Polo." There were two T-shirts behind the bar advertising the Kill a Gar Festival. One showed the front, the other the back, with this running downward: Rod and Reel, Blowgun, Crank Telephone, Pistol, Dynamite. Crume said, "Hey, Stet." He wore a crisp starched white shirt and a tie. He kept his cell phone in front of him, next to a vodka tonic. "I'm down to 1,194 of these things." He took off his Hole in the Head and handed it to me.

This is when I read all those patents, et cetera.

I didn't say, "You don't look like one of the locals," or "I did some research and there was a real company back in the sixties that mass produced these things; nowadays there's a product that looks like a regular foam rubber visor for kids to wear in the bathtub." I had some training. The edges of this particular Hole in the Head weren't smooth, and looked as though they might could cut skin. I said, "I'd be willing to bet that your father lost his mind at one point."

The bartender came up to me but didn't say anything. I said, "Shot of bourbon neat. Can of Pabst, if you got it." He stared at me about five counts too long. He'd seen some David Lynch movies, I imagined, unless Waterloo held a foreign film festival right after the Kill a Gar fiasco.

Billy Crume might've been forty years old. He said, "It must run in the family. I just got fired last month." He looked down the row of regulars and said loudly, "Was it last month I got fired, Starling? I got fired right after you got let go at Fuji."

I thought, Fuji—film developers. Groundwater-tainters and eco-terrorists, now all glum for not inventing the digital camera. I thought, This is the right place to be.

Starling said, "Two months."

"I got fired two months ago. I worked for the highway department. The South Carolina Highway Department. Came up with a way to knock out the roadside littering. You probably read about it." I balanced a Hole in the Head where it belonged. Sure enough, it scratched my brow. "I'm the guy who decided to throw bags of garbage out along secondary roads, with fifty and hundred dollar bills inside somewhere."

I said, "I read about it. I have to admit that I didn't go around looking, though. Bed of my truck's usually filled with rocks."

"If it'd worked I could've either gone straight over to run DHEC, or gotten a job with one of the finer advertising firms," Crume said. "It should've all worked, man. People think there's money out on the ground, they go along the roadsides picking it up. They figure, As long as I'm out here, I might as well throw this other useless garbage in the back of my truck so I don't look through it again next week. When they find money, they get hooked and look for more. Next thing you know, we got us some clean-ass highways in the state, and new industry comes along wanting to relocate here, and then everyone's employed, the tax base goes up, the school's get better, our students go off to fancy colleges and learn how to act right. By that I mean, not to throw their garbage on the side of the road."

Billy Crume said all of this really fast. I could tell that he'd said it, daily, for some time—probably more than two months. The other men stared ahead. Starling, who had the same head shape as a Beluga whale, said, "Blueprint didn't include death, whether accidental or not."

My tape recorder ran. The bartender brought me a shot of bourbon and a can of Budweiser. I didn't correct him. "My blueprint didn't include death, whether accidental or not," Billy Crume said. "Maybe Darwin was right, as it ends up. Maybe the fittest *were* meant to survive. Least fit looking through garbage, and picking up litter on the side of the road, in hopes of getting some money. More fit own cars, get distracted, swerve, and kill the least fit. That's how that little experiment worked out. And on top of that, I think those people above me—my bosses, the higher-ups in bureaucracy—never really put money in the middle of litter. Next thing you know, the people not being killed on the side of the road are going home mad, gathering up their own garbage, and throwing it out on the roadside. Or in front of the South Carolina Highway Department in Columbia."

No one responded. Billy Crume either finished his story or waited for a question. Me, I had learned growing up that southerners will tell a *stranger's* stranger just about anything, if they feel smarter about a subject—from growing crops to textile league baseball stats, literature to homeopathy—that it'll make them feel bigger, and more important. I said, "Can you eat gar?" like that, my voice coming out a little higher than I wanted. Most people told a recipe for gar that was similar to the one for carp: clean the fish on a plank of cedar, throw the wood on a grill, then eat the cedar.

Starling said, "Yes."

"I can't tell the difference between gar and salmon," Billy Crume said. The men didn't look at each other with a twinkle in their eyes. They didn't smirk, or laugh.

I thought, Either you guys haven't ever eaten a decent meal and wouldn't know the difference, or you've perfected a kind of you-can't-make-us-feel-smarter-than-you master improvisation best known to seasoned politicians, lawyers, and firecracker manufacturers sneaking under the Bureau of Alcohol, Tobacco, and Firearm's guidelines in regards to cherry bombs. I said, "Did your father ever sell enough Holes in the Head to make a living? How'd he come up with the idea?"

Someone honked a horn outside in the parking lot. No one looked toward the door. No one walked in presently. "My mother took to selling Tupperware. Having Tupperware parties, you know. My father might've been the first husband to ever set down a Tupperware lid atop a hot stove eye. That's the answer to your second question. Number one: No, he didn't make a living at it. He secretly made four of the little shields, then made me, my brother, and two sisters wear them to school. We walked to school. He drove behind us to make sure. I don't know why he thought little kids in school would go home and say to their mommies, 'Could you please purchase a Hole in the Head from Mr. Crume so I don't get shampoo in my eyes at bath time?' That's not how kids work. We should've worn the things to Tupperware parties, if anything. Couldn't do that, though, seeing as he manufactured the things secretly, so my mother ended up going 'Where did I put the lid to the lettuce crisper?' you know, when it came time for her to show off her products."

"She left my daddy soon thereafter," Starling said. He didn't turn his face.

Crume said, "Could I get another one, Mike?" to the bartender. "She left my daddy soon thereafter," he said to me.

Mike said, "My father took me down to the DMV and left me, so a more suitable person could bring me up a orphan. My daddy said I was tarnished."

I looked at Billy Crume to see if this was his next line. He didn't say anything. The orphan story seemed to be Mike's, and Mike's only.

Three men left. It didn't appear that they paid their bills, and I didn't see Mike mark up a tab. "You have no plans on buying any of these things, do you," Crume said. Outside, someone honked what appeared to be the car horn from earlier. The sun sank enough to make it difficult to see the lake, or the parking lot.

"I'll buy one or two. I'll buy three—one for me and my wife, and one for our child who won't be able to use it for a couple years, seeing as he isn't born yet."

"Well," Crume said, "I guess that's better than none. Hardly worth the gas to come down here."

Starling said, "You know it's a conspiracy." He picked up his can of beer and held it to his temple.

Crume got up from his stool and said, "You know it's a conspiracy. The way gas prices have gone up. See, gas goes up so high, the newspaper deliverer has to quit his job. It ain't worthwhile for him to break even, or flat-out lose money. Then normal people don't know what's going on 'cause they don't get a daily paper. The government can plan out all kinds of things, and normal people like you and me won't know what's going on, unless we have a computer."

"Poor normal people ain't got computers," Starling said. He swapped temples.

"Poor normal people ain't got computers," Billy Crume said. "Hell, if they can't afford a car to go buy their own newspapers from down at the closest newspaper stand, they ain't going to have computers to read what's going on. So now the government can pass any crazy law they want—especially if it has to do with their friends in the oil business, you know. And to keep people like me—who have to advertise in the want ads—from making any money, keeping a newspaper subscription, maybe buying a computer and keeping up with what the hell's going on."

I said, "It's a brutal cycle. I know what you mean. We're pretty much doomed."

"If I were you," Starling said—or at least that's what I thought I heard—" then 'dick' would be 'duck.'" It took me until Billy Crume came back inside with three Holes in the Head and a stack of T-shirts to figure out that Starling had said, "If 'I' were 'U,'" like that.

Crume said, "If I were U, then 'Fizz' would be 'Fuzz.'" He placed his load down at the end of the bar and unfurled a few shirts. "Here's another little business venture we came up with one time. Can't sell it over the Internet because none of us has the Internet. Can't sell it through the newspapers for the same reason, we found out, that we can't sell them at the jockey lot.

I guess around South Carolina there's a little thing called the Obscenity Law which has longer arms than the goddamn First Amendment."

"And it costs too much in gas to drive to another state, or go all the way down to Myrtle Beach where those special shops sell novelty shirts and whatnot," Starling said.

Mike brought me two more drinks without my asking. When I look back on things now, I think about how I had kind of forgotten all about the story of Billy Crume's father, and so on. Crume said, "All the way down to Myrtle Beach."

I got up and walked to the end of the bar. There I read a white T-shirt's slogan: If I Were U, Then Pissy Would Be Pussy. Another one read If I Were U, Then Rim Would Be Rum. I said, "Shit would be shut. If I were U, then 'Shit' would be 'Shut.'"

"Yeah!" said Billy Crume. Then he and his buddy Starling went through a litany of what they'd printed up in the past: Sin Would Be Sun, Gin Would Be Gun, Lick Would Be Luck, Bitter Would Be Butter.

I said, "I'll take two of those shirts, too. You got maybe a large and a medium? I'll take the Fizz Would Be Fuzz variety."

Billy Crume said, "If 'fick' was a word, we'd've made a killing. Or gone to jail for pornography." He said, "They ain't but six dollars apiece. Let's finish our drinking and then I'll get you some out of the trunk."

I sat back down half-blind from glare coming through the windows. Both Starling and Crume talked, I would find out later when I listened to the tape recorder. Mike continued some of his story about being left at the DMV as a child until somebody understood that he was too young to get his permit. My head filled with only one thing, of course: If I Were U, Then High Would Be Hugh. If I Were U, Then Click Would Be Cluck. If I Were U, Then Sickle Would Be Suckle.

"You still with us, Stet?" Crume asked me.

"If I Were U, Then Huck Finn Would Be Hick Funn."

"That's right," they said. They drawled it out: "Da-a-a-a-t's... r-i-i-i-ght ...." I felt as if I'd been initiated and accepted invitation into an exclusive club for conspiratorial idiots. "If I were U, then we'd all live in South Caro*lun*a," Crume said.

Bitch Would Be Butch, I thought, but kept it to myself. As an adult low-residency master's program Southern Culture Studies student I understood that it might offend someone, somehow, no matter what, of course, even here surrounded by dead gar inside He's Out Casting.

I don't usually place my head down on a bar counter and fall asleep, at least not around strangers. So when I finally stirred back to life I could only think that maybe Mike had snuck something in my drink. Or it could've been the effects of too much sunlight in the bar. Those shellacked gar snouts kind of emitted an odor not unlike that found inside an old person's house, and God knows I can't even drive by a nursing home without feeling sleepy.

My tape recorder had stopped. I'd gone through one and a half two-hour cassettes, and the fourth hour ended while I snoozed, evidently. "Get this old boy another shot of your bourbon," I heard Starling say.

"Get this old boy another shot of your bourbon," Crume repeated right after.

I kept my eyes closed and listened, head turned toward Mike's shelves. Right after he set a shot glass under my nose, I heard him say, "It's past four-thirty. Big Time can have a beer now."

I feigned being passed out still and tried to remember if one of the other regulars from earlier had been called Big Time. Mike drank with us all afternoon, so it wasn't as if he could only drink late in the afternoon, when he adopted some kind of pro wrestler moniker.

I lifted my head and opened my eyes when I heard someone slapping the bar nonstop, and making a noise normally heard as part of a Tarzan soundtrack. "Sorry, there, buddy. We didn't mean to disturb your dreams," Starling said.

Next to me, around the ell of the bar, stood what ended up being a Bonnet macaque. At the time I only thought, There's a monkey at the bar. I didn't have time to focus on genus and species or whatever, and outside of orangutan and chimpanzee and lowland gorilla, my ability to identify members of the ape family was rather limited. It's not a subject that comes up in Southern Culture Studies very often, I doubt, even in regular residential programs.

Of course I jumped back off my stool, grabbing my bourbon, and said, "Whoa, man." The macaque yawned. Its eyeteeth might've been three inches long. The monkey slapped the bar some more as Mike poured a can of Pabst into a Styrofoam cup.

"We didn't mean to disturb your dreams," Crume said. He now wore one of his T-shirts. It read If I Were U, Then Tricked Would Be Trucked. "Don't worry none about old Big Time. She's a girl. She's friendly."

"She gets friendlier once a season, as do all the girls in the troop," said Starling, which Crume repeated.

I got all confused thinking about Girl Scouts before I remembered what a pack of monkeys called themselves, instead of a herd, knot, covey, or clutch. Mike set the cup down in front of the monkey and she pooched her lips way out, head craned above the rim. Big Time's eyes darted mostly toward me. I said, "I won't steal your beer," just in case she understood English. I didn't want the thing leaping unannounced toward my jugular. I'd seen documentaries.

"We call her Big Time because we thought that's where she'd eventually bring us," Crume said. I downed my shot of bourbon and tapped the glass on the counter twice for more. "You remember how those late-night shows always had special animals on there, like that tree-climbing dog Flatnose from down near Darlington? Well we thought Big Time would take us there. She can catch a gar. A lot of people don't know that monkeys can swim and dive like the rest of us, but they can. And for some reason Big Time here—when we first got her she went by plain Mary—took a dislike to garfish about as much as the rest of us. Half the heads on the wall were caught by Big Time. She's what gets us the Grand Prize every year. Most Gar Killed. Biggest Gar Caught Alive, you know. *By hand.*"

I reached in my pocket, pulled out the last cassette tape I'd brought, and popped it in the recorder. I hit Record. I said, "Start over." The macaque finished her beer, then sat back and stared at the window behind Mike. I said, "Does she need to wear diapers? Can she use the toilet? Where the hell did y'all get a fish-catching monkey in the first place?"

Starling laughed and said, "That'll cost you."

Crume said, "Where else in the whole United States do you think grown men sit in a bar learning about what may or may not be their distant cousins? That'll cost you. Two rounds for us, and one more for Big Time."

I pulled out my wallet, and then listened to a strange tale about Billy Crume's older brother ending up in India somehow, hiring locals, going out into some dense forests and capturing a half-dozen Bonnet macaques, sending them back illegally aboard a sloop, breeding them in what used to be a bear enclosure bought from some Cherokees up in North Carolina, training the things to be comfortable around humans, then setting them free to roam Waterloo's environs.

Starling began talking for me, somehow. He said, "Bullshit," right before I did.

"OK, you got me," Crume said. "Here's what happened. I'll swear on a stack of Bibles here, or upside down ones in Australia. Somebody down in south Florida set free some of these things back in 1930, and the next thing you know they're all over the place. My brother went down there some time ago. Back and forth, all the time. I won't say why, but I'll say that he told on his employers and now my brother's somewhere in Idaho or Wyoming with a new identity. Anyway, one of these trips he took some live traps and a special bait he said came to him in a dream. Next thing you know, we got so many monkeys on chains that we ran out of chains and let them loose."

I thought, I've heard this somewhere before. I thought, Monkey on a chain—one of my other supposed subjects for a low-residency Southern Culture Studies master's program essay mentioned monkeys on chains, didn't he? I watched Mary—Big Time sounded like a pimp's name to me—sit stunned from the beer. She stared at all the bobbers on the ceiling, and I wondered if her monkey mind told her she sat in a cherry tree. I said, "That's a good story."

"Won't be for long," Starling said.

Mike wiped up where Mary dribbled on the counter. He said, "Y'all know I close up early on Wednesdays. Got to take Leanna to church since she can't drive no more."

"Won't be for long," Crume said. "I might just have to crawl into a knothole and die when the monkeys disappear."

Even slightly drunk and tired—and I'll admit now that maybe I feared both sitting there, and sprinting to my truck in getaway mode—I had no choice, as a hopeful Southern Culture Studies scholar, and as a matter of etiquette, but to say, "Why." Then I put my hand over my glass so Mike the bartender couldn't fill it again.

Billy Crume placed a Hole in the Head atop his pate for no obvious reason. He pointed toward woods south of He's Out Casting. "Giant federal prison being built thataway," he said, then pointing more toward where I'd be driving home, "and a new landfill that the state of South Carolina has agreed to hold every other state's toxic waste will take up a couple thousand acres spread across thataway." He put both hands down to his side, but continued wearing the plastic shield. "Monkeys go one way, there'll be no valid habitat. They go the other way and I'm sure what sentries don't pick off with their rifles, the inmates will. We been trying to capture the rest of them, but not all the monkeys are as tame, smart, or far-sighted as Big Time."

"Then there's the paper mill," Starling said.

"Then there's the paper mill," Crume said. "Oh, they say they plant trees in the spots where they cut one down, but it takes years to grow a good tree for a monkey to climb. This lake will die off from no visitors, and the monkeys will die off from no hand-out peanuts."

Mike opened the register, didn't count the paper bills, and shoved them in his front pocket. He said, "I'm sorry, fellows, but y'all have to get out of here. I'll call up my cousin and tell him to turn his head. He's patrolling up and down 221 right now."

Mary turned her head toward me. I'd read about that gorilla learning sign language, but I'd never heard about a Bonnet macaque learning how to speak English. Maybe she just yawned again, but the sound she emitted came out almost like those orphan tribal kids saying, "Can't you afford just twelve cents a day?"

I didn't ask how much. I didn't ask for a leash or a cage. Arbor Day neared. A gentle beer-drinking monkey seemed like an appropriate gift for a pregnant wife.

Big Time Mary jumped right into the passenger seat and sat down forward, as if she'd been for a ride before.

I am not the kind of man who insists that he drives better while drunk, or slightly drunk, or stoned, or slightly stoned. But I believe that I drove between the lines well, and ten miles under the speed limit—my eyes focused directly on the pavement ahead—for the first half of the fifty mile drive home from He's Out Casting. I didn't look at Mary. I didn't talk, or respond to her slight chatter.

I imagined Abby running down the steps from our rough-hewn house, smiling, her speech impediment miraculously cured, excited on my bringing a monkey into our fold, and how our newborn-to-be would have an instant playmate way out where we lived on the Unknown Branch of the Saluda River. I could hear Abby saying, "If she's used to plucking gar fish out of the water, I'm sure she'd be a quick learn for picking out flat rocks—maybe you can start the river rock business back up. Maybe you can soothe your dead father's soul by not letting the family business dwindle into nonexistence. Maybe you can patch up some good faith with the landscape architects who once trusted your not haphazardly running off to study Southern culture ..."

I worked hard to concentrate on the road, but I daydreamed in a way that ancient hunter-gatherers must've visualized coming home.

I looked over at Mary and said, "If I Were U, Then Sicker Would Be Sucker," and then to myself said, "Oh, man. I get it."

So much for reverie. I wondered what Billy Crume would've pulled out for sale had I not taken the monkey. How much farther could he go? And at that moment, halfway home from Waterloo, I foresaw Abby leaving me altogether—going to live with her parents until the baby was born, until I resold the monkey. And then I foresaw Abby not moving back home whatsoever—she'd go further north, maybe to Minnesota, in order to lose her dialect and impediment, and in order to raise our child far from a region of the country where it wasn't impossible to take over the miserable and unlikely lives of monkeys every day. In a way I underwent a study of South America.

And then I foresaw orphaned Big Time Mary being pregnant, and having a baby that I could only name Jesus. Word around my nearly impassable part of the county would spread, and anti-Darwinians would come out of nowhere, catch Mary, and injure her mightily. I would have to take one of the Holes in the Head and place it gently over Mary's bulbous skull until her wrenched neck healed adequately. She would drink beer endlessly to quell the pain, develop an addiction, and somehow drown in the river beside my house, leaving me with the orphaned Jesus that I wouldn't have patience to train, and who would wander off imprinting himself on any arboreal creature the woods had to offer before I could get him to the Department of Motor Vehicles where, I'd learned, strangers claim the tarnished.

Billy Crume and Starling, eventually, would come find me, make more offers, perhaps some threats. I would sit alone on the front porch, the Unknown Branch of the Saluda River flowing louder each year in such a way that could only cause tinnitus in both ears. Then I'd either go back on the road with a trunk full of ammunition in order to assassinate anyone I didn't think voted correctly in regards to the environment, or I would shove a barrel mouthward, heave my legs up until I was fully fetal, and use both big toes to pull the trigger.

It would be my final salute to Southern Culture Studies.

I turned down my long rutted red clay driveway and saw Abby ahead, walking back from the mailbox in the half-dark. She turned to me, smiled, and held a manila envelope up. Dr. Crowther, I knew, had sent another assignment for my completion before I returned for the final one-week residency down in Mississippi. I went ahead and stopped the truck, got out, and held both hands up in submission, keeping the door cracked so the dome light worked. I breathed out hard, in hopes of releasing the last traces of the day's booze.

Abby said, "Did the interview go well? Did you get a story?" She wore a loose-fitting cotton sundress with red polka dots. It looked like the ceiling of He's Out Casting.

Then her eyes locked with the monkey's. Mary waved at my wife. I said the interview went about the same as the others. Abby asked where I got the cat.

I THINK I HAVE WHAT SHARON'S GOT

WHEN THE GUY CALLED saying he was my brother, or half-brother—or ex-half-brother, in a way, seeing as my father'd died—I said, "Yeah, yeah, yeah, I've heard about this scam, buddy." Who hasn't?—it's been all over the news for years. I hung up the phone. I had other things to worry about. I had a girlfriend who said I'd better propose at the two-year anniversary of our dating. We were at the twenty-third-month mark. She said at two years she'd go from being either a fiancée or an old girlfriend, either one, it didn't matter to her. Who would want to marry that? is my question. Who'd want to get legally hitched to a person—man or woman—who lived off of ultimatums? I'd quit living with ultimatums right after this rich born-again guy said he'd back a documentary I wanted to make if and only if I could find a way to have Jesus Christ come out as the hero in the end. Up until this point I'd only finished up two short documentaries, both of which won awards at little film festivals—which I was pretty proud of at the time, basically because I didn't know that every film won either a Platinum, Gold, or Honorable Mention in one of about two hundred categories—in places like Charleston, Lubbock, Asheville, and Johnson City. One of the films was about a woman who saw a picture of the Virgin Mary—this is going to get kind of grotesque, I'm sorry, I'm not making this up—on one of her feminine napkins. It wasn't a tampon, or one of those big cottony things. It was one of those thin feminine hygiene deals with the strip of glue on the other side. Looking back, she had a boyfriend or husband who had a college degree in art, and I'm thinking he might've used some food coloring and drawn that Virgin Mary outline. He might've been proficient in watercolors, I don't know. My other documentary was about a group called Pistols for Politicians. They kind of advocated shooting congressmen who backed the Second Amendment. These P for P guys kept arguing that there were no handguns when the Constitution got written, and that all that "right to bear arms" crap would've been reconsidered had Thomas Jefferson and the rest of those guys foreseen how nobody goes deer hunting with a nine millimeter Glock. This was two hundred years before we even tried to convert to the metric system, for one. So there's that. There's that problem, with Francie. Somewhere along the line she read where people had to get engaged right at the one-year mark.

Before the stuff with my half-brother, like about a week before, she accused me of either throwing away her clothes piece by piece, or adding hangers in the closet so as to confuse her, make her think she's going crazy. She came in one day saying "I just finished my laundry, and all my clothes are hung up, and there are two extra hangers. Am I missing something? Am I missing some of my blouses? Or did you decide to be nice and buy some extra hangers? Was there a big broken box of hangers that came in on your job and y'all divvied them up?"

I work in the middle of the night loading and unloading trucks. It's only six hours a night, but I get paid decent money and have health insurance. I figured when I took the job that I'd only keep it until I was on my way with the filmmaking. There'd been talk that the Carolinas would be the new Hollywood. I read it somewhere. I figured, when I took the job, that I could still make documentaries in the daytime. Who makes documentaries at night? Answer: Filmmakers who have come across people who think they're vampires. I'm not interested in vampires, or werewolves, or those other night-only people, even though that's when I work.

I said, "I haven't been stealing your clothes, Francie. I'm not into that. And I haven't gotten ahold of any hangers. Is this your way of saying I'm not contributing to the household? I can get hangers, if you want. I'll put it on my list. I'll write it down below flood lights, smoke alarm battery, and birdseed. And bird feeder."

She said, "I'm not saying that. I'm just saying."

I said, "Saying what?"

She looked liked she might cry. She said, "What about these!" I'm talking she kind of yelled it out, then whipped these little snapshots from her back pocket.

I looked at them. They were pictures of the last long-term girlfriend, a woman who *never* wanted to get married. Her name was Rubecca, like that. Rubecca. Her father's name was Ruben, and her parents had a girl. I used to kid her that it was too bad her father didn't marry a woman named Ella, and they named their daughter Rubella. That would be a cool name, I always said. It would be like getting named Measles, or Polio, or Mumps.

Rubecca had always said, "Rubella is measles."

I said to Francie, "Where did those come from?"

I'd never seen them before. It's not like I had a stash of photographs hidden away of ex-girlfriends. I didn't even own a dirty magazine or porn movie anymore.

I looked at the pictures. Rubecca stood in front of various cages at one of those petting zoos on the side of the road. This was down in Florida, where we went to school right in the middle of the state. Orlando was going to be the new Hollywood. My high school counselor had told me that one, and Rubecca's counselor told her that, too, all the way up in Ohio where she was from. What are the chances of two high school counselors—one in South Carolina and the other in northern Kentucky where everyone says they're from Cincinnati—saying something like "Hey, if you want to go study how to make movies, forget about NYU or USC. Orlando's the new Hollywood!"

I flipped through the pictures and saw Rubecca in front of the world's largest alligator, and in front of an emu, and in front of a wild boar. It wasn't much of a petting zoo. You couldn't really touch any of the animals. Maybe I spent too much time taking pictures and I missed out on the pygmy goats and llamas and pot-bellied pigs, I don't know. The photos got taken right about the time Rubecca and I graduated, before we moved to western North Carolina, where we heard they'd be hiring cameramen and whatnot for all the movies that would be made there. That big-time movie about the Civil War guy walking across North Carolina trying to get home on the mountain?—that got filmed in Romania. I might've missed some kind of news article on how Romania was the new Hollywood. I thought only vampire documentarians went to Romania.

Rubecca was not unattractive. I'm talking she could've gotten a job in any number of those Cinemax movies. You could hide an Etch-a-Sketch sideways between her boobs.

I said, "I've never seen those pictures in my life. I swear to God, I've never seen those pictures in my life."

"For your information," Francie said, "when I was looking around your closet for my clothes, I came across one of those throwaway cameras. I took it to that Jack Rabbit place, and here's what came back."

I said, "You know what? You know what? First off, you should be able to tell that those pictures were taken something like thirteen and one-half years ago. Second, What would you say if I went snooping around the boxes in the bottom of your closet? Tell me again why you're all hopped up on getting married?"

Francie had a regular job. I'll give her that. She could've had any other kind of man who didn't have dreams of still working in the industry. She could've gotten married to a veterinarian. Most people think I'm about to say she could've married a doctor or lawyer, but I say veterinarian for a reason, which has to do with my half-brother or ex-half-brother.

I tried to hand the snapshots back, but she said, "If thinking about her when we make love helps you keep it up for more than an egg timer, then maybe you should keep them."

Francie worked for the chamber of commerce, trying to convince people that they should move to western North Carolina, or why they shouldn't leave. Maybe I had developed a skewed way of looking at things over twenty-three months, seventeen of which was living together—and maybe it's how the world ends up evened out somewhat in the ways things work—but it seemed like Francie came home most days trying to convince the ones *closest* to her to *leave*.

By the ones closest to her, I mean, of course, Sharon the Dog, and me.

Sharon the Dog got named by Rubecca, though I've never explained it all to Francie. I had Sharon for nine years before Francie and I met, plus a year between Rubecca and Francie, then the twenty-three months. Sharon wasn't full-grown when she showed up one day, but she didn't have puppy teeth, either. She was one of those dogs, the ones who just show up a few months after Christmas because some kid wanted a puppy, and the parents said "Only if you take care of it," and the puppy never learns to pee on newspaper, and the next thing you know the dog's taking a ride in the passenger seat of the family car. Rubecca named the dog after the movie star. Sharon showed up running across the road, then got on her belly and crawled up across the lawn to me for the final thirty yards or thereabouts. Then she rolled over and lifted one leg way up in the air. She might have arthritis now, but up until she was maybe ten years old she would lay on her side with one leg up in the air. She looked like she had semaphore down. In a previous life, Sharon must've been on the high school flag team, or the starter at a stock car race. What a great dog, even with arthritis! She had the body of a smallish black Lab, and the head of an Airedale, or Irish terrier. She had one of those scruffy muzzles, is what I'm saying.

But then she got old. She got old, and she started having problems with her digestive system in a way that most dogs don't. Sharon didn't seem to ever *use* the bathroom. I'd long before taught her not to go past the yard's boundaries, so it wasn't difficult to walk around both front and back yard looking for evidence, you know. She didn't seem to be getting all that bloated—like you'd think a non-evacuative dog might get—but it certainly affected her spontaneity, and her energy level. When she stretched out on the floor, none of her legs poked up in the sky.

I might've noticed all of this a lot sooner, but six or so months before the half-brother arrival Francie was feeling particularly romantic and she said, "You might want to have a dermatologist check out that thing on your back. You might have skin cancer."

It's not like we were in bed with some kind of mirror on the ceiling. And we weren't off swimming in order to get exercise, seeing as I sometimes moved about 18,000 pounds from one conveyor belt to the other overnight if it comes out right that I average fifty pounds per minute. So I didn't need to swim. It was nothing like sex or swimming. I'd merely walked out of the shower.

I said, "What? What're you talking about?"

The next thing you know, I'm finding out that sure enough I do have pretty good health insurance—I mean, I had to go to the dermatologist three times before I passed the deductible, but that's not so bad, considering. Not everyone on the street can go to the dermatologist. I thought about going around with my camera and asking people on the street—and they're the ones who need to see a dermatologist, more than anybody, I guess—when's the last time they had a melanoma checkup. I never did, mainly because I'm kind of nauseated by people's skin afflictions.

That, and after pulling nearly ten tons every night I couldn't lift a camera to my eye socket.

So I went to this dermatologist and he checked out the mole on my back and right away said, "This is nothing."

I said, "Well, get it off of me."

And he said, "OK. This might sting a bit," but it really didn't. He took a can of what looked like compressed gas duster and froze the thing. It came off in the shower a couple weeks later. No problem. Unfortunately, the doctor looked all over my torso and then put on some kind of special glasses and stared at this thing that might've been the size of a tick's pecker. He said, "We're going to have to keep an eye on this one."

"Which one?" I asked him. It was on my shoulder, right on top. I looked down and barely saw it. If I'd've seen this thing on Francie's shoulder I might've said, "Hey, did someone come down to the chamber of commerce and get pissed off about this not being the new Hollywood, so they stabbed some pencil lead into your shoulder?" It was that small.

The dermatologist said, "Yes. Yes. Yes, we're going to have to keep an eye on this."

But he didn't take a picture. I've seen them take pictures on TV shows of things they got worried about. Maybe I should've taken some pictures of the mole every week, then hid the throwaway camera in my closet. Later on—maybe after I was dead from skin cancer—Francie could find the thing and get it developed, et cetera. But I'm not that way. She might do it, but I wouldn't.

Now maybe I've explained enough. These are the kinds of things I had going on. Possible skin cancer, a beautiful ex-girlfriend who never wanted to marry me, a constipated dog that I loved, something about either missing clothes or extra hangers, and a deadline with Francie. I'm a little obsessive, and what's leftover gets taken up with paranoia. I understand that. The documentary that I wanted to film way back when that the born-again guy wanted to back if and only if I brought Jesus into the picture?—it was about a guy who tried to wainscot his entire mountain house interior with Popsicle sticks, but midway through the process he started thinking about diabetes. I guess

I could've talked the guy into forming some kind of cross-like pattern on his walls, but—even then—I had other things troubling me. I forget them now, and I'm sure they had to do with Rubecca, but I'm sure that other things invaded my thoughts.

I'll be the first to admit that maybe I'm not the only one in our little house with these other things on his or her or its mind. After all of these setbacks and hurdles and roadblocks—the last one being the mystery hangers and photos of Rubecca—Francie said, "Hey, that half-brother of yours is on his way over. I forgot to tell you. He's on his way. He called, I answered, and he's on his way."

Well I had nothing else to say except, "Are you crazy? Are you crazy and trying to take me down with you? You know better than to give out our address to strangers. This guy might be one of those Africans saying he's got a fifty million dollar bank account stashed away, and he needs our help. He might be an Amway salesman. He might be from a religious cult. He might be selling vinyl siding."

I went on and on. I thought of some more things, but I didn't say them. I thought of some mean things, like how maybe this so-called half-brother was really a traveling man of the cloth who could wed us, and there was nothing scarier than that, at least until some things changed. But I didn't say it.

This was a Saturday. Francie said, "He already has the address. He said he's seen you before and that y'all look alike. He said he's been running into you for a while now, and he's bringing some documents to show how y'all's father was the same man. What's the story with your father? Did he travel or something?"

I said, "I don't know. A long time ago I heard him slip up and say how his first wife had to be institutionalized. I thought he only tried to scare me. And Mom."

I let Sharon outside, because she could still bark when anyone came close to the front door. I watched my dog from the window. She went outside, and sniffed. She sat down and watched a bird fly overhead. She got up and peed, but nothing else. I said to Francie, "This is not good."

Francie said, "Maybe after your brother leaves, you can take me to a petting zoo. I'm sure that I like animals as much as your other girlfriends."

Ten minutes after I let Sharon back in, my half-brother showed up with two bottles of wine and a fifth of bourbon. So maybe we were related, I thought right away. We looked alike only if we stood at opposite Fun House mirrors—like if my mirror stretched me out a foot, and his mirror made him kind of wide. Francie stood looking through the den window as the guy walked up. I still wasn't convinced whatsoever. Francie said, "Y'all have the same ears and foreheads."

Anybody could say that. Outside of maybe one of those tribal people with the giant holes in their ears and Frankenstein's monster, about everybody had the same ears and foreheads, if you ask me.

I went out the door. I stood on the stoop, but I didn't smile yet.

My half-brother walked up saying, "I know this is crazy. I know it's insane. I've been knowing about you since you were in high school, but I didn't want to bother you. Sometimes I think those shows where unknown siblings show up out of nowhere—I think those people feel as though they're being bothered."

I said, "Hello."

He put two bottles of wine beneath his left armpit and kept the bourbon in his left hand. He stuck out his right and said, "I'm Morgan."

That was my paternal grandmother's maiden name, I knew. But anyone could take a Detective 101 class and get on the Internet and learn all that stuff. I wasn't convinced. I said, "Zack." I said, "Listen, anyone could take a Detective 101 class and get on the Internet and learn all that stuff."

Morgan had me by a good fifteen years. He was healthy looking, but he had to push fifty. He leaned his armpit my way and said, "I didn't know if you and Francie drank red or white. And I brought along some bourbon, too. If we're related, about two glasses of wine only gets us thinking about the harder stuff."

I took the bottles. He held up an index finger for me to wait there. He ran back to his car, one of those new Jeeps that isn't really a Jeep, and came back with a photo album. Francie came outside and stood next to me. Already I could tell that she was taking his side. She said, "You can't get a photo album off the Internet. I mean, I guess you can buy somebody's on eBay, but unless you sold yours to a stranger, this is going to mean something."

Morgan came back and shook hands with Francie. She told him to come on inside. I'd never seen her so proper and hospitable in our one and eleven-twelfths years together. I expected her to point out where we keep rope and duct tape and the sharpest knives. Francie said, "Tell us all about yourself! Have a seat right there and I'll get some glasses. Do you want the wine or the liquor?" She went on.

Morgan sat down at the dining room table, which was really just a table in a room that was part of the den. It's not like we had a separate room for dining. He said, "I know this is strange, Zack. You can tell me to leave if you're uncomfortable."

I said, "I'm always uncomfortable. Don't get the wrong idea by my demeanor."

I don't think I'd ever used the word "demeanor" in my life.

Morgan cracked open his photo album—I half expected to see some pictures of Rubecca in there, after everything that had happened within the week—and pointed out, sure enough, a bunch of old photographs of my father with another woman, with another baby (Morgan) and another car (Fairlane). I said, "That's my dad, all right."

"Let me see, let me see!" Francie came in squealing. She'd brought in wineglasses, a platter I'd never seen before, an ice bucket I'd never seen before, two regular squat glasses, and a bowl of mixed nuts. "I love seeing pictures, even of people I don't know."

I looked at her like she was out of her mind. But I didn't say anything. I didn't want Morgan to get the wrong impression.

Then Morgan turned some pages to photos that looked like me when I was ten, then twelve, then fifteen. They were pictures of him, of course, but you could see the resemblance. He said, "From what I've pieced together, my father married my mother. My mother became mentally ill and had to be institutionalized. I was brought up by her sister and her sister's husband, from the age of two. My parents got divorced, my father met your mother and got married some eight or nine years later. I guess it was still a time when families tried to hide their mentally disturbed relatives. My mom and dad—who were really my aunt and uncle—never mentioned anything while I grew up. When I was home from college one time I went up in the attic to steal a smoke, you know, and I came across the photo albums. There are more. When I asked my parents, they told me the whole story, then they made me promise not to seek out my biological father. These were really devout religious people. They said it was meant to be otherwise if and only if God came down and said I should seek out my biological father."

I poured bourbon into two glasses. I put a cube of ice in mine, and looked to Morgan. He took his neat. I said, "Please don't tell me that God came down and spoke with you."

Morgan started laughing. He shook his head. "No. I guess I was just getting lonely for a sibling."

I said, "Please don't tell me that you have some kind of rare, incurable disease that's genetic, and you had to come find me to say I didn't have much time left."

I waited for Francie to say, "Oh, God, yes, please don't say that you have a rare and incurable disease." She said, "I have some cheese and crackers I'll go get."

Sharon came in from where she liked to curl up in the bathroom next to a vent. She wagged her tail and walked right up to Morgan without barking. I said, "And you got yourself a half-dog in the deal, I guess. That's Sharon."

Morgan got down on the floor. He got down low, and put his face right up to my dog's. He said, "I'm a vet. I'm a veterinarian." Then he started talking like people do when they talk to dogs. Sharon let out one bark, but kept wagging her tail. She collapsed in front of Morgan, rolled over, and stuck that one leg up in the air like in the old days.

"A veterinarian!" Francie came back into the room saying. "I work with the chamber of commerce, and we were talking the other day about how we could use more vets in the area. We could use more vets, doctors, nurses, and policemen. We don't need more banks or insurance agencies."

Morgan said, "And you, Zack—you work for UPS, and you make films. I'm glad one of us turned out all right."

I couldn't tell if he was being sarcastic. What was that supposed to mean? I couldn't tell if this new half-brother was some kind of smart-ass. Why would a veterinarian make fun of himself as not turning out OK? I said, "Well, I haven't finished a documentary in some time. But I have ideas, you know. I was thinking about doing something about the tattoos that people have where I work. This one guy says he has a hitchhiking hobo tattooed high up on the back of his thigh, so it looks like his thumb is catching a ride with whatever's coming by. That might be too gross. And I can't prove this one at all, but I've noticed how the local news has an anchor guy named Keith, a sportscaster named Kevin, and a weatherwoman named Kelly. You see what I mean? Three Ks. I'm wondering how many small-town local news outfits have a KKK offering up the day's happenings. I think it's on purpose."

I wasn't sure if Morgan listened. He finally got up off the floor. He said, "How old's Sharon? Ten or twelve?" I told him. I said, "She's been a great dog. But to be honest—I'm glad you're here—I think she's kind of stove up. She doesn't seem to be using the bathroom."

I couldn't think of the correct vet-talk. I said, "She's not defecating regularly. There's nothing out there in the yard, and she doesn't run off. She's not one of those needs-to-hide-in-a-bush dogs."

Francie sat with an unusually upright posture. Was she flirting? I half-expected her to go change into something more comfortable, like some see-through panties and nothing else. Francie said, "So you're not a vet around here, are you?" Morgan shook his head. "Down in Augusta. My parents moved to Georgia early on, and I went to school there and stayed. I've come up here I don't know how many times thinking I'd pop in, but I kept losing my nerve."

I couldn't get that I'm-glad-one-of-us-turned-out-all-right out of my head. Who shows up out of the blue and makes fun of a just-discovered sibling? Answer: Nobody who is sane. I wondered if Morgan took after his crazy mother.

Morgan sat back, took his glass of bourbon, and drank it down in two gulps. He poured himself another. "I know what's happening to Sharon," he said. "I've seen this happen before. She's eating her own feces. Somehow you've just gotten out of sync with seeing her defecate. She's old, she's gotten kind of bored, she's probably a little depressed, and she's eating her own excrement. It happens, as they say."

Francie said, "Ugh." Francie said, "I let her lick my face all the time."

I felt as if Morgan accused me of boring my own dog. I said, "I don't know."

My half-brother shrugged. He said, "Nothing new. Nothing to be embarrassed about. Put some garlic in her food and she'll probably quit doing it."

I opened up the photo album and looked at photographs of a boy who looked like me playing golf, standing on a roof, feeding fish in an aquarium, sitting stoic-faced with what appeared to be a purebred retriever. I said, "My father never showed up or anything?"

Morgan said, "Oh, he showed up. He was Uncle Zack. He showed up about twice a year, then once a year. Then he didn't show up. But don't judge your father. I have a feeling that my parents asked him to quit coming. And I'm almost sure that I was named Zack and it got changed."

Sharon sauntered over and put her head on my leg. I tickled beneath her chin in a place that caused her to raise her lip on one side. I looked down and saw nothing stuck on her teeth. This Morgan guy might be all wrong, I thought. I thought, He probably only deals with poodles, down in Augusta, where everyone places golf.

Francie said, "Are you married, Morgan? Do you have any children?"

"Here we go," I said. "Francie says that I have thirty days to pop the question. She has some rules she must've come across in one of those books."

Morgan said, "Was. I have two children but they live with their mother during the school year, then with me summers. Boy and a girl, eighteen and sixteen. My son's the oldest one, and he's going off to NYU to study filmmaking in the fall. My daughter has her sights on the same path. It's the weirdest thing, but both of them are deathly afraid of dogs. Preachers' kids go wild, and I guess veterinarians' kids rebel in the only way they can figure out."

"I'll be damned," I said. I looked down at the opened album. There I was again sitting in a VW. I said, "They're saying that New York's the next Hollywood." What else could I say? I sat there. I looked at the photo album but didn't turn pages. I bet my heart didn't beat more than twelve times a minute. For the first time ever I realized that I wasted way too much time, didn't follow dreams, and wouldn't have minded dying.

"I just hope that my kids don't end up bored like their old man. I work mainly with chickens. I used to have a practice where I dealt with dogs and cats, but somehow I strayed into working for all the poultry industry, more or less. There's a documentary you need to make, Zack. When I ever retire—and I won't be able to until the kids get out of school—I'm turning those chicken fuckers in. It's inhumane. I don't want to get all high and mighty like my parents, but y'all don't want to eat any chickens unless they're free-range. Trust me on this one."

He gulped his bourbon, but didn't pour another. Francie said, "The way you said that, at first I thought you meant that bestiality went on."

I looked at her. Somewhere between the trips to the kitchen and back she'd pulled her hair back into a ponytail.

Morgan reached over and pet my dog. "Compared to what I'm paid to inject into those poor things, they'd be better off. At least they'd be getting some exercise. If there's such a thing as reincarnation, you don't want to come back as a chicken, I tell you that. Or a vet with a conscience."

I thought Morgan might cry. Of course I didn't know him at all, so maybe he couldn't hold his booze. Finally he said, "Well. Well, I better get on the road. It's almost a four-hour drive. I better get on the road."

I didn't know whether to ask him to spend the night or not. I would do it the next visit. And I didn't know whether to shake his hand or hug him like a brother. I didn't know whether to watch or look away when Francie hugged him, either.

But I knew this: I would quit my three-to-nine a.m. job within two weeks. I'd tell Francie. She'd move out and get a much better place to live, maybe one of the new townhouses with a view of the mountains. If she didn't go down to Augusta on weekends and begin a relationship with Morgan, she'd at least scope out a local veterinarian who had the ability to get all choked up over chickens. That would be fine. I'd not blame her whatsoever. I would take what money I'd saved up, plus what I had socked away from inheritance money, and go full force into what I meant to do in the first place. Maybe I could find a way for Morgan to take a hidden camera into some of those chicken factories. Maybe I'd film a sequel to the Virgin Mary woman, or the Pistols for Politicians members who eventually got arrested for one thing or another. I'd come up with something. In between slowly rolling a ball to my dog so that she didn't get bored, I'd come up with something.

DURKHEIM LOOKING DOWN

THE ORIGINAL PLAN for the evening didn't involve talk of symbolically drowning the Father of Sociology, or of finding ways to live without neighbors. It didn't include four quarts of the cheapest wine found in the grocery store aisle, either. The two couples were to meet at an Applebee's halfway between, eat dinner, then drive together in one car to a lecture. Afterwards, they'd go back to the restaurant, have a nightcap, then leave. Russell Hamby and Connie Bratcher taught together at a social science magnet high school filled with upper-middle-class kids who swore their allegiance to receiving grants from all the humanities foundations later in life, after attending Stanford, or the University of Wisconsin, or Berkeley, though everyone knew that the students' parents only cared about their children getting into top-tier universities so that they could brag about it later, but send them to the University of South Carolina in order to study international business, economics, accounting, and so on. Russell and Connie taught sociology. They'd been hired together six months earlier. Connie worked for the Department of Social Services before, and Russell had taught sociology, American history, and driver's education and coached the girls' tennis team at a traditional public high school with a 40 percent graduation rate. Russell and his wife Trina had sold their home in Mount Pleasant a few years earlier and moved onto a houseboat they kept on the Ashley River. "If it comes up, please don't tell them why we had to move to the houseboat," Russell said to his wife as they drove to the restaurant. "I mean, tell them all the good reasons why we're there, but not the reason why it makes you feel safe."

Trina turned down her visor. She exhaled and said, "Oh, I won't. I know how important to you this Connie woman is. I wouldn't want to come off as a crazy." She looked straight ahead. "Why're we going to a fucking Applebee's? Six thousand good seafood restaurants in Charleston and we're going to a neighborhood chain. And then a free lecture. What, are you and Connie giving yourself some extra credit?"

It was Connie's husband who had suggested their meeting place. Derrick figured that at least there would be a television nearby showing a college game. Even when they returned to the restaurant at ten o'clock, probably those West Coast teams would be playing. Derrick renovated historic houses in downtown Charleston. That's what he told people. In truth, he was a meticulous master carpenter who got hired out, who got recommended word-of-mouth, who hadn't driven a nail outside a four mile square area in ten years—between Broad and South Battery Streets. On the way to meet the Hambys in Connie's car—she didn't want someone suggesting that they all pile into her husband's work truck later—Connie patted her husband's leg and said, "Thanks for doing this for me. I owe you. Next time there's a homebuilders show at the civic center, I'll go with you."

"I'll let you hold my ball peen later," Derrick said. He kept his left hand atop the emergency brake as his wife drove.

Connie said, "I think Russell's wife might be a little on the gossipy side. We might not want to bring up the no-bark collars. I mean, I have no clue why the subject might come up, but we probably don't need to tell them about the collars."

Derrick said, "If she starts talking about those rich neighbors of theirs at the marina, maybe I'll bring up how she needs to wear one."

Connie didn't respond. She flipped up her visor, as did Derrick, once they turned out of the driveway. A mile down the road she yelled out "Damn it," and turned into a strip mall parking lot. "I set the bag out and then I forgot the things."

Derrick wasn't listening. He tried to think of possible topics of conversation for the evening as Connie drove them back home. He'd built custom-made cabinets for a psychologist one time, for instance. A sixteen-penny nail once shot out of his nail gun into the flyway of a houseboat where he'd been commissioned to build bookcases, a captain's table, and a wet bar.

When his wife returned from their house with a paper sack of tomatoes Derrick said, "Are we going to their house? Applebee's has enough vegetables, I'm believing."

"No. This is the whole point of going to this guy Gerry Core's lecture. Remember? I told you. He's on the bestseller list and everything. He bills himself 'Mr. Pompous.'"

Derrick thought, If Russell wants to talk about electric shock therapy, I can kind of talk about that.

Russell and Trina waited outside. When Connie and Derrick drove by them in search of a parking space, Connie asked her husband to roll down his window. She wanted to let Russell know they'd be a minute. Derrick pointed to a space ahead. Connie yelled "We made it!" into the inside of the passenger window.

They sat boy-girl-boy-girl out of habit. Connie faced her coworker and Derrick faced Trina at the high, round table. Because they didn't want to be late for the lecture, Russell told the waitress they'd take the first available table, which ended up being in the smoking section half of the bar. Behind his head, Derrick caught snatches of the Florida-Georgia game being broadcast.

Trina lit a long cigarette. She said, "I guess it's only a matter of time before I have to steer our houseboat halfway into the

Atlantic in order to smoke a stab." Derrick turned around to see a replay of an interception. "I'm sorry," said Trina. "I'll blow it away from you."

Derrick shook his head. "No, no. It's not bothering me. I used to smoke, too," he said. Derrick couldn't decide if Trina looked like a moll or a model with her lips pursed. "Nowadays when I get the urge ..."

"I read on-line that Gerry Core started sitting behind chicken wire at his readings, then he changed to Plexiglas. They say his insurance company dropped his policy," Connie said, loudly, to Trina and Russell. She interrupted her husband before he could say that he chewed tobacco when he had withdrawals.

Trina ordered two martinis—"Not one double, two separate"—and water in the special three-foot-high glass usually used for draft beer. She asked for no ice. Russell and Connie ordered merlot, Derrick two shots of bourbon and a Coke chaser. Trina said, "Thank God someone besides me likes to drink."

The play-by-play announcer said, "No—you can see it from this angle that his knee never touched the ground. That's a fumble, my friend." Derrick fought to remain focused on his wife.

"And he *wants* the tomatoes," Russell said. "You remembered to bring tomatoes, didn't you? Overripe plums would be good, too. But no one should be throwing rocks or bottles. That's what caused Gerry Core to use a barricade in front of him. After his appearance in Boston. I can't wait to hear what he says about Charleston. We brought two dozen eggs."

Connie nodded. "He's such a masochist. You're right. You've got it right. What you said at faculty meeting was right," she said.

Both Derrick and Trina, to themselves, wished that one of their spouses would explain *exactly* what would be going on, or who this Gerry Core man was. Neither wanted to appear ill-informed or outright stupid. Derrick got enough of that, he felt, for simply being viewed as a manual laborer. And Trina—what went through her head? Russell wondered daily—only rotated between channels that aired self-diagnosis programs ever since her doctor and lawyer deemed her too obsessed to be employed successfully.

Derrick lifted his wine. "May we never become as pretentious as Dr. Core." They clinked glasses. Because the waitress never brought an ashtray, Trina tapped her cigarette into her water. Derrick said, "Let me get you an ashtray," mostly because he wanted to turn and see the score. "You'll end up forgetting, and then drink nasty water."

Trina said, "I'll never drink water until it's probably too late."

A local car dealership commercial for people with bad credit popped on as Derrick looked up at the television set. After stepping to the horseshoe-shaped bar and returning to their table, Derrick noticed that Trina wore shiny silver panties, and that she sat with her legs fairly open. He thought, Are those made of aluminum foil? He placed the ashtray in the center of their table and sat down. Everyone looked at the menus. Derrick motioned to the waitress that he wanted two more drinks and a new water for Trina. Then he said, "I know that I might not be the best husband around. I'm guilty of coming home from a twelve-hour day renovating houses—or houseboats, I've worked on remodeling houseboats, y'all—and maybe not listening to everything that Connie says. I know that she and you, Russell, think your principal Roy is a little man with a tiny brain, a chip on his shoulder, and a smaller pecker."

Trina laughed. Connie said, "Derrick. Come on. You're a perfect husband," but she smiled at Russell.

"I try to listen, I swear." Derrick held up his right hand. Russell stared at the calluses. "For the life of me, though, I can't remember a single word about this professor we're going to see. Somebody fill me in. Somebody point the caulk gun my way."

The waitress brought Derrick's second round. She reached over to the bar and got the water. Both Connie and Russell changed over to mojitos. Connie said, "Yes, you sometimes don't listen."

Trina threw up both hands in the air and said, "Oh, goodie. They have *nachos* here! I don't know how we'll never become pretentious or pompous what with *nachos* on the menu! Fancy! And *look*—one of those deep-fried *onions*!"

Russell said, "Be a good sport, honey."

Connie said to her husband, "Maybe I didn't explain Gerry Core. I thought everyone knew him by now. He's been on *Oprah*, like, four times."

Dr. Gerry Core never taught at the same university for three years in a row. His various department chairs evaluated him, always, "Though Dr. Core knows his subject matter ..." and then enumerated how Core came across as aloof, spoiled, audacious, haughty, competitive, irrational, short-sighted, stubborn, narcissistic, elitist, inflexible, overbearing, demeaning to both students and colleagues, and—oddly—charming "in his way." Core didn't trust the shades of grading, and gave out only As and Fs, nothing in between. In one particular nineteenth-century British literature course he only lectured on the importance, and beauty, of tiled floors. In a twentieth-century American lit class he asked that students learn how to fashion a variety of paper airplanes, then held contests as to distance and time airborne. He *requested* to teach the entire seven volumes of *In Search of Lost Time*. The students that semester—this was in Chicago—met three hours a week at a nursery school, and amid the whines and wails of babies Dr. Core lectured on the nuances of child labor laws around the world. Then, finally unemployable, he handwrote a list of aphorisms down, got the thing published from the same people who put out 365 *Ways to Cook Beans*, 365 *Ways to Fix Chinese Leftovers*, 365 *Ways to Spice Foods When Herbs Are Unavailable*, and so on.

The publishing house had a young, eager, and competent publicist. Gerry Core hit the talk show circuit, then the campus circuit, and more than a few of his epigraphs got printed on paper coffee cups around the country.

He became a cottage industry, for he predicted that everyday people—that is, people with only college educations, or doctorates from state-supported universities—*needed* to hate someone, *needed* to release their hostilities, *needed* to say to their friends, "That Core guy might be rich and famous and intellectual, but I'm still glad to be me."

"Whatever anyone does here, please," Trina said after exhaling smoke slowly into the middle of the table, "please don't order fajitas." She scanned the menu. "Or anything else that might arrive on fire."

Derrick looked at his wife looking at Russell. Connie said, "I don't pretend to know much about pop culture—I guess if I had a subspecialty, then it'd be pop culture—but Dr. Core, I think, has learned how to bring a reality TV show right to a city near you every night."

Derrick tried to listen to the game. One of the refs either pulled a hamstring, or had a heart attack. The fans booed him.

Russell said, "They say he spoke at last year's NEA convention." Russell looked at Derrick. "National Education Association convention. Core evidently started right off with 'One who can't do anything in the real world ends up teaching. Those who cannot teach become administrators. Those who cannot administer turn to selling real estate.' He got fucking *pelted*."

Derrick looked at Trina and said, "I'm not even hungry, to be honest. Maybe I'll just get some cheese sticks. They're not flammable." To Russell he said, "I know what the NEA is. There's also the National Endowment for the Arts. I've been on television twice back when *This Old House* came to Charleston. I was in the background, but they talked about my 'superb craftsmanship.' That's what they called it. 'Superb craftsmanship.'"

Connie said, "Russell wasn't saying it that way, honey," though she knew that he did. "You could probably get an NEA grant for your work."

"I should apply," Derrick said.

Trina kept looking at the menu. She used her finger, going down the entrees. "How did y'all exactly meet?" she asked.

The waitress appeared and asked, "Are y'all ready to order?"

Everyone looked at Trina. She said, "I wouldn't want them blaming me for being late to see this asshole speak. What's the fastest thing on the menu? I don't mean like, a chicken can run faster than a pig. I mean, what would come out of the kitchen quickest."

"Probably a salad. Any of the salads. Or the nachos. Even the nachos grande."

Trina nodded. She said, "I'll take the penne pasta with the Italian sausage gigantesco off to the side." She refolded her menu like origami. "Sometimes I feel like I need a big old sausage gigantesco."

They all ordered the penne pasta with Italian sausage gigantesco, though Connie had been trying to stay away from anything resembling a cured meat, and didn't particularly enjoy anything slightly anise-flavored. "We've known each other since college," Connie said.

"Before college. We met at the orientation. They made us do some kind of ropes course long before anyone else did those stupid kinds of things. I wanted to make a noose and hang myself," Derrick said. He tipped one of his glasses of bourbon into the other. He picked up the Coke, then set it back down. "What about you and Rusty?"

Connie kicked him. He always called Russell "Rusty" whenever Connie brought up something daring that Russell mentioned at a faculty meeting. Russell didn't seem to catch it. He said, "When we throw the eggs, remind me to aim right or left of Core. I believe I'm getting a buzz."

Trina leaned in toward Derrick. She raised her eyebrows and smiled. Derrick made eye contact, but imagined those silver panties of hers. He planned to drop his napkin or knife when their food arrived. Trina said in an exaggerated whisper, "The whole reason we live on a houseboat is because I might spontaneously combust one day. I need to be as close to water as possible." She jerked her head once in the direction of the tall water glass.

Russell put his hand on his wife's right forearm. He said, "I was lucky enough to have met Trina working at the history museum. I'd go down there and just stare at the Gatling guns, you know. And then at the Hunley submarine when they pulled it out of the ocean. Trina here told me how I could become a member for cheaper than buying a new ticket every time."

Trina held her head back and opened her mouth, but she made no noise. Connie stared, then she picked the linen napkin from her lap and rearranged it. She noticed that one of her buttons was undone, pretended to cough into the napkin, and quickly fixed the problem. "This was before I couldn't take it anymore," Trina said. "This was before the doctors agreed that I was a late bloomer in the world of bipolarity. Bipolarity's no hilarity, let me tell you. That's what they say at those support groups I go to."

Derrick said, "Huh."

Connie's napkin fell to the floor and she asked Derrick if he would get it for her. He looked at the button she'd rebuttoned. Trina said, "What's your specialty, Connie? You said you had a subspecialty. What's your specialty?"

Connie was the only one enough in her right mind to drive—Russell surmised that some medication he took must've mixed improperly with the wine, then rum. They ran late, and therefore sat in the front row of the Dock Street Theatre. Russell and Connie thought of it as fortunate: How hard will it be to hit the guy? Trina walked with a slight limp, Derrick noticed. He wondered if she always favored one leg over the other. "This won't be good, believe me," Derrick said to all of them when they got settled down. Everybody in the audience stomped their feet in unison. "This is going to be like being in the chicken bone section at Darlington. *We're* going to get hit by tomatoes, I guarantee you."

No one came out to introduce Gerry Core. He walked out from behind the curtain and stood in front of the microphone. There was chicken wire *and* an eight-by-eight foot plate of Plexiglas shielding him from the audience. Core nodded. He cleared his throat. He wore a red tunic and a safari hat. His white hair sprang out from behind his ears. Because Charleston is known for a series of houses down on the Battery called Rainbow Row, Core started off right away with, "People who live in houses painted pastel to look like Necco Wafers have the aesthetic sensibilities of the dung beetle."

People laughed. One tomato grazed the top of the shield. Core didn't smile. He continued with remarks targeted toward these particular citizens. "If you have carriage rides in your town, then you will have horse shit on your streets. If you have horse shit on your streets, then your children will always be slow in terms of potty training, not to mention modern conveyances." No tomatoes hit the stage. Core loosened his shoulders a few times. "OK. How about this—any citizen who brags about having retained a slave market in the middle of his village 'for historical purposes' is like someone who brags about having retained an abscessed tooth. Why is it that anyone who demands a Confederate flag flying in sight for historical reminder never thinks to burn his own house down every day in remembrance of General Sherman? Why is it that all you Baptists down here believe that Jesus hated trees? Quit making those paper religious tracts and handing them out."

A full-scale attack occurred. Core didn't seem to be bothered, affected, or caught off-guard. Because they were still boy-girl-boy-girl at the theater, and because Derrick felt that his wife and her colleague were pretty much hypnotized, he leaned into Trina and whispered, "I hope he doesn't say anything bad about women wearing silver underwear. I might have to throw a tomato if he says anything derogatory about women wearing silver underwear."

Trina nodded. She let one side of her mouth curl up. "Fire retardant. They're fire retardant. That might not be the politically correct word anymore. They're fire mentally challengedant."

Derrick squinted both eyes and nodded his head. He turned back to his wife, who booed. The professor had made a disparaging remark about arts festivals, of which Charlestonians prided themselves. Gerry Core said, "Oh yeah? Well listen to this: Modern dance is to ballet as slam poetry is to literature. And in regards to furthering humankind, a person who writes original compositions and plays them on his comb-and-toilet-paper poor man's harmonica—that person is far more valuable than anyone playing, say, Mozart or Haydn by rote."

Audience members filled the air with a variety of objects, but only an empty Perrier bottle hit the stage. Core smirked, undeterred.

Connie turned to Derrick and said, "Isn't this fun?"

Russell put his arm around Trina. "Now I remember why I never drink. If someone threw grapes I'd go up there, stomp on the things, and make more wine." He held an egg in his left hand. Nothing Core said, so far, angered him, or made him rethink his life.

Gerry Core drawled out in a fake Southern dialect, "I got here last night and toured your city. I talked to people born and raised here. I'm not sure that I can say everything I need to say in one lecture. Just because you *live* and *talk* in an historical district doesn't make you important. Listen. People who *teach* history wrongly believe that they *make* history. On a side note, people who *teach* sociology never understand that they're the most *unsociable* of the worker ants."

Connie and Russell leaned back and heaved their first projectiles. Derrick and Trina didn't urge them on, for they believed that Dr. Core said something that they'd not been able to put into words over their respective marriages. And if the evening with Gerry Core ended here, perhaps there would've been a heavy emotional cargo stacked unevenly, listing these two relationships in particular.

But Gerry Core—as if personally knowing his audience members and their insecurities—said, "A man who relies on his hands to make a living—boxer, carpenter, pianist, mime—must understand that *nose-pickers* rely on their hands, too."

Derrick didn't know his ambidextrous abilities until he launched two tomatoes one after the other, splattering the Plexiglas so well that Core had to lean to one side in order for the audience to see him say, "Want to discover the missing link? Look to people who live on houseboats."

Two security guards came out of the wings in order to escort Trina off the stage, and out of the Dock Street Theatre. While she waited for her husband and Connie and Derrick, she read a plaque outside. She read how Junius Brutus Booth—father of John Wilkes Booth—tried to kill his manager here in 1838. Before her group arrived, she thought, Junius Booth tried to kill a man here, and I tried to kill a man here, which made her, for the moment, forget about spontaneously combusting in public. No, instead, she thought, I'm famous.

"That man might be right up there with Einstein and whoever invented the smoke alarm," Trina said in the car, "but I'm still glad I'm me. I'm glad we're us, you know."

Derrick drove back to the Applebee's. He promised that he'd sobered up enough. He adjusted the rearview mirror a little at a time until, while passing under streetlamps, he caught flashes of

Trina's protective underwear. He said, "How much did y'all pay for those tickets?"

Russell coughed. He rolled down his back seat window an inch. "Trina can't drive in the first place, and I don't know if I'd be safe on the road. Would y'all mind coming by the houseboat for a while?" He looked at his wristwatch. "It's still early. We can stop and get some wine or beer. I'll buy."

Trina said, "Russell."

"Come on. It'll be fun. I can call a cab and get our car in the morning. It's locked." Russell sat behind Derrick. It didn't seem right; it felt awkward to all of them. If anything, didn't two men usually sit up front in these situations? Derrick thought.

Trina said, "Russell."

Connie turned around. She said, "I don't think I've ever been on a houseboat. Let's do it. Can we? I hate to impose. Lord knows that goddamn Gerry Core would say something about our being an imposition. I've never been on a houseboat."

Derrick said, "I thought you had a thing about barnacles."

"I'll buy beer and wine. And some chips. Wait. We have pretzels at home. I'll get some bread and cheese. Take a left up here so we can hit the Piggly Wiggly. Teach that pompous Core a lesson in sociology. I'll get Velveeta and white bread. Smoky links boiled in grape jelly. Ripple. Boone's Farm wine. He has no clue how provincial we can be."

Derrick waited at a stoplight. He thought to say, I've seen your car at the marina, Connie. Don't lie to me. You've been on a houseboat—you've been on *Russell's* houseboat. When Trina must've been off at her psychiatrist's, or getting electric shock treatment, or visiting a meat locker in order to stave off combustion. But Derrick opted for, "Mad Dog 20/20."

Derrick said nothing else. He might've been wrong six months earlier. More than a few people drove Jettas in and around

Charleston. He never got close enough to examine the license plate. Derrick had forced himself to look away, to drive back to his job. On that particular afternoon, he remembered, he replaced six newels on three staircases. He had carved his initials into their bases before screwing them in.

Russell said, "It doesn't take long to do a tour." They stood in the middle of the houseboat. Russell pointed to one end and said, "Two bedrooms and one bathroom. He pointed out that they stood in the den, then rotated slowly to show the kitchen, dining room, and flyway.

Connie said, "When did y'all get this?"

Derrick said to himself, Don't mention how this is only a mobile home trailer on floats. Trina finished putting beer in the refrigerator. "Hey, Derrick, I got a stash of bourbon. You want some bourbon? I want some bourbon." She reached beneath the sink and pulled out a bottle of Pine-Sol. "Don't worry. I washed it out before I poured it in."

Russell sat down. He said, "Well this explains some things," and Derrick noticed how his voice sounded different—higher, kind of sing-songy. "That big refill for liquid hand soap's really tequila, isn't it? No wonder every time I shake hands with Senor Perez he starts laughing."

Everyone else sat down. The den looked as though it had been shipped directly from a Wood You showroom of minimalist furniture. Derrick thought, There's fabric missing from this relationship. There's wood, but hardly any fabric. Connie wanted to know where they got fresh water. She drank a glass of strawberry wine and said, "I'd have a hard time bathing in salt water every day."

No one corrected her. No one explained the situation. Derrick looked at a framed photograph of angular, downcast Emile Durkheim on the wall. Connie kept the same picture in their laundry room. Durkheim had a giant moustache, and in his own way looked like a riverboat captain, Derrick thought.

The day after Connie brought her framed eight-by-ten into the house and nailed it to the wall, Derrick went straight to the encyclopedias in another man's house where he finished up some work on a marble countertop. Durkheim, Derrick learned, pointed out that we lived in a state of anomie—that the rapid change from traditional to modern society could only cause deviant, normless behavior. Suicide played a prominent role in Durkheim's thoughts. Derrick wasn't sure if he liked Durkheim, and he wasn't sure why Connie wanted him to be reminded of normlessness in the laundry room.

Trina got up, retrieved the Pine-Sol bottle, and placed it on the table. She sat on the armrest of Russell's chair. "Tell us something strange about y'all's marriage, Connie. Derrick. Come on. We're all adults. I told you about how I used to catch whatever disease or phobia I saw mentioned on TV."

Russell forced a laugh. "Well, honey, you didn't tell them until just now."

"OK. So. Now it's out there. I saw a show about the history of people who burned internally until they turned to ashes. Except for their feet. Feet don't have enough fat. They don't work like wicks." Derrick stared at Trina. So did Connie. Russell stared out of a porthole. "Therefore, anyway, we moved here so I could jump right in the water. That's my strange story."

"I don't think it's all that weird, Trina," Connie said, though she didn't sound convincing to anyone. "When I was a little girl my mom forgot to put sunscreen on me. My skin got so burned that it bubbled. I guess I thought I might catch on fire."

Trina stood up. She shook her head from side to side. "No. Not the same." She lit a cigarette. "Blisters fill with water, and that would put you out."

Derrick thought, Maybe I should go ahead and tell them about the no-bark collars we wear to bed. Connie would kill me, he thought.

Russell said, "My turn! Well. Let me see how to put this. OK, I'll come right out and say it: I used to be gay. I mean, I guess technically I'm still gay, but not like before."

"Yeah, like that," Trina said. "Something strange about your relationship that no one knows. Or hardly anyone knows."

Derrick reached over for the disguised bourbon. He read on the label "Disinfects." Maybe it wasn't Connie's car over here after all, he thought. He thought, It's a good thing I didn't come out and lambaste her for it. He said, "I have nightmares that Connie's leaving me for you, Russell, and I scream in my sleep so loud that I had to start wearing a shock collar. And then on top of that Connie grinds her teeth, and sometimes it's so loud it somehow *sets off* my collar. So she had to start wearing one, too. That's our story."

Russell, evidently feeling comfortable enough to allow some flamboyance to seep out, said, "Kinky." He held his eyebrows high, his mouth in an O, and looked back and forth from Derrick to Connie.

Connie said to Trina, "Should you be smoking? What if you inhale a spark?"

"What if she causes a flame, *like me*," Russell said. "I've said it before. Lord knows if I smoked around her she'd say I tried to induce her death."

Derrick got up and went for the tequila. He said, "Can we take this thing down the river and into the harbor? I believe old Emile might want to go for a ride. All that talk of individual consciousness and whatnot." Derrick pointed at the photograph. "Let's take the boat out for a ride, and throw him in the water."

No one knew how to move the houseboat. Russell said that if a hurricane came through and they were asked to move inland, he'd have to hire someone. "And then where would we be? We'd have a stranger with us, somewhere on a river near a swamp, probably wanting to molest Trina."

"I bet he's staying at the Francis Marion Hotel," Connie said. "We should go over there and let him know some things about us."

The others looked at her. "Our future houseboat captain?" Trina asked.

"Gerry Core," Connie said. "I guess that's the fanciest hotel we got. You know he's only going to stay in the fanciest hotel."

Derrick drank from the hand sanitizer bottle. He said, "I don't need a lemon or salt. I'm betting that the soap had a lemon tint to it in the first place."

Trina crossed and recrossed her legs six times. She said, "Tell them about your idea, Rusty. Tell them about the ice. The blue ice."

Derrick closed his eyes and imagined driving the house boat out to open water. In his mind he saw Emile Durkheim beside him, wearing a captain's hat over his bald head. He envisioned crashing the boat onto a reef-encircled island, then having to resuscitate Trina and Connie. He saw Russell floating on a piece of wreckage, swept to Cuba by the Gulf Stream.

He opened his eyes when Russell said, "This would be *delicious*." Derrick got up from his seat, walked to the photograph of Durkheim, and eased the wire away from its hook. He brought the photograph back to his seat and held it on his lap. No one said anything about it.

Connie said, "We could use the lobby phone and order him a bunch of cheap wine from room service. No! We could pretend *we're* room service, and attack him right there in his room. Tie him up. Torture him. Not, like, kill him, you know, but torture him."

Russell held out one palm as if taking an oath. "I was thinking about making these giant blocks of blue ice. I guess I'd use either some food coloring, or even Kool-Aid. They have one of those tropical flavors now that comes out blue. Anyway, I was thinking about making these giant blocks of blue ice, then finding a way to crash them through one of our neighbors' roofs. It's getting too crowded around here, man. I could catapult them through all these neighbors' roofs, and pretty soon people would think that we were living beneath a flight pattern, you know, where jets dump their sewage. Y'all've seen that blue ice, right? Like that woman in Nebraska or some place that had it crash into her living room?"

"Blue ice has human waste in it. You'd have to add some things to your blocks of ice to make it lifelike," Derrick said.

"I told him to eat a bunch of beans, get gas, swallow some bullets, drop his pants on the flyway, and shoot the neighbors," Trina said. "Who's going to check for gunpowder residue down there?"

Derrick stood up. He held the picture of Durkheim in his left hand. "Man. I'm telling you. You should just drive this boat somewhere else. I'd move it everyday and drop anchor."

Connie said, "I'm tired. Are you tired, Derrick? This has been fun." She stood up. "Thanks for all the beer and wine. We need to do this more often."

Trina kept sitting. She said, "We're not really going to kill any of our neighbors. Tell them we're not serious, Rusty."

Russell said, "We have an extra room if you want to stay. Y'all stay. Come on! I'll fix my famous waffles in the morning." He looked at his watch. "I can do that right now." He walked over toward the stove.

"No, I have to work in the morning," Derrick said. "I'm behind on a house over on Prince."

Derrick concentrated on not wavering. He took his wife by the elbow. She said, "And I promised to help him," which wasn't true.

"Goodnight," Trina said. She pulled her skirt up and flashed them repeatedly. "Goodnight, goodnight, goodnight" she said, as if it were her fire-retardant panties speaking.

Derrick didn't want to go back in the houseboat when he realized that he'd taken the picture of Durkheim with him. He placed it in the back seat, upright in the middle, like a phantom passenger. He drove out of the marina slowly and said, "If we started eating dirt and talking to dogs, we wouldn't be as strange as those people. I'm sorry, Connie, but your buddy there is messed up. So's she. We might wear no-bark collars to bed at night, but at least we're not them."

Connie didn't respond. She directed Derrick to the hotel where she felt certain Gerry Core, right about now, would be sitting at the bar, drinking brandy, or cognac. She said she had some things she wanted to say to him. She had questions, too. "Everything's that man's fault," she said, at first loudly, but then as she repeated it—as Derrick drove in the opposite direction of their house—she barely remained audible.

I FEEL LIKE BEING NICE TODAY

EVEN WITH MY LIMITED interaction with Randall Minning, I knew that he was the kind of man who shouldn't drink bourbon and talk to strangers. I had arrived an hour earlier than my lab partners and waited at a table for the rain to let up. Randall came in looking loaded for bureaucrats and sat down hard at Gus's Riverside Informal Tavern. Gus had just put out a new sign and said over time he might change it to True Gus's Riverside Informal Tavern so it came out True G.R.I.T. At the time I couldn't know that Randall Minning brooded about his wife Donna back home, eight miles away on the other side of the Saluda. This was July, and it looked as though God finally decided to parole the drought that left us a foot below normal yearly precipitation. Last year we went something like nineteen inches, and the year before that it was sixteen. It had rained, according to Gus, six inches in the last twelve hours.

Randall Minning left his house, he mentioned right off coming through the door, with the ceiling dripping and his wife insistent that she could see an angel's image on the splotchy sheetrock. She didn't want him to go up and patch some faulty nail heads, seeing as a wet angel looking down had to be some kind of good luck. Randall Minning turned to us and said he didn't believe in angels. He believed in tripolymer sealant.

"When I was in college I worked as a roofer four straight summers," he said to Gus. "Four straight summers is enough to understand that you don't want to make a career out of that. At

least that's what I thought. I had this sissy roommate who studied
Spanish. You know what he does now? He's a Spanish-speaking
gun-for-hire making a lot of pesos when he's contracted out by
the courts and police and anyone else who wants to translate
something into English. More power to him, I guess. Every
day there're more people wanting to understand something in
English."

"You went to college?" Ben Joe Purcell asked. He was the only
other patron at Gus's, and sat a few stools down from Randall. I
pretended not to pay attention, but it was impossible. Nothing
good could ever come out of these two men talking. Ben Joe
wore a Harley-Davidson hat, as if he'd ever been on anything
more powerful than a moped. But he always wore a hat in order
to hide the scar.

Randall Minning pointed toward his empty glass. Gus poured
in two shots. The tin roof sounded as if someone was pouring
marbles onto it. Randall Minning stared at the rain beyond the
plate glass window behind the bar and said, "I don't know why. I
went, I graduated, I didn't conquer."

If Donna had seen angels more often on the ceiling, and if
Randall escaped his house each time before taking a crowbar
and beating his walls, then he'd have known that Ben Joe sat
on this stool most afternoons, pontificating. Ben Joe drank
from Gus's opening at noon, and usually walked home around
three. Before his accident, he worked as a bitter adjunct English
instructor at the college, tearing down everything printed in the
required anthology while trying to get his own dreadful work
published. I'd had him my second semester. Everyone knew that
it only took "I completely despise the work of William Faulkner,
Flannery O'Connor, Eudora Welty, and the rest of these writers,"
to make a solid A in Ben Joe's class.

"If I had to do it all over again, I'd've gone to veterinary school
over in Georgia," Ben Joe said. He turned forty-five degrees
toward Randall Minning. Then he moved over one stool. "I

would like to get to the bottom of how dogs speak to one another through their eyes."

Something told me—and I figured Gus knew, also—that this was how Ben Joe's "accident" started. He had moved over one stool—then another, and then another—toward a man wishing both personal space and solitude.

Gus said, "Don't get started on that again, Ben Joe."

Randall Minning said, "Ben Joe, or Banjo?"

"Ben Joe. It's a nickname that stuck. I had cousins who couldn't say my name right, and that's what came out of their mouths."

Gus came around his side of the bar and brought me a PBR without my asking. I thanked him. He said, "I'll just run a tab until your friends show up."

I said, "They better."

Ben Joe Purcell leaned toward Randall Minning and said, "Let's say a dog goes for a ride with you. Wait. You got two dogs, and one of them goes for a ride with you in the car. Y'all pass horses and cows, maybe a couple old dogs standing on the side of the road, you know. Then when you get back, the dog you took will go over to the dog left behind. The second dog will make a noise that means 'Where'd you go?' And the traveling dog is able to bring back pictures of what he saw in his pupils. You see what I'm saying? The dog that went for a car ride will bring back images of the cows and horses and stray dogs along the way, kind of like a photograph's negative. We can't see them. People can't see them, but dogs can. I don't think cats can see them either, but dogs can. The scientists know all about it. Police forces and the FBI are trying to get the government to allot more money per year to the scientists, so that some time in the near future if a dog sees a crime happen, we only have to go look into the dog's eyes and see the perpetrator."

I looked down at the Formica-topped table, and didn't need to look up in order to imagine the look on Randall Minning's face. He said, "Are you out of your fucking mind? What're you talking about, man? Listen. I don't know which issue of the *National Enquirer* you read that in, but it's my advice for you to cancel your subscription."

Ben Joe pulled his head back. In a high, whining voice, he said, "All right. OK. If you don't have an open mind about these things, I guess I understand."

He turned and looked straight ahead. Gus went back behind the bar and said, "December 24, 2000," which was the date when a still-at-large man tired of listening to Ben Joe's crackpot notions went outside Gus's, got a tire iron, and hit Ben Joe upside the head.

I figured that Randall Minning—if he wanted—could get up and throw Ben Joe Purcell through the plate glass window. I thought that anyone around here must have heard about Randall Minning and been in his presence a couple times. He was big—at least six-five, 230 pounds—and reportedly had the only genius IQ in the county. He'd worked as some kind of think-tank guy for everybody from the Democratic National Committee to Greenpeace. He'd been hired out by the environmental people to do some things to land developers. He'd been prosecuted, defended himself, and come out with the judge declaring a mistrial.

For as smart as Ben Joe claimed to be, I couldn't believe that he didn't recognize Randall Minning. Maybe the knock to his head caused some kind of recognition/memory malfunctions.

Randall Minning said, "I feel like being nice today," loud enough to give Ben Joe a chance to understand that he meant it. "I'm not going to throw you through the plate glass window, retrieve your unconscious body outside in the rain, then drag you down to the river and drown you."

Randall Minning pointed out the back window and nodded for Gus to look. I stood up and looked, too. Ben Joe turned the other way, as if needing to inspect the pickled eggs. Two men wearing camouflaged ponchos stood by the river, both holding fishing rods. The rain came down sideways. Tree limbs across the river swirled in giant Os. Gus said, "I'll see those two boys every day for the rest of my life, I'm betting. One caught a thirty-pound catfish down there couple weeks ago."

Randall Minning ordered another bourbon, plus a can of Schlitz—which I didn't even know Gus sold. I guess I would've ordered Schlitz, too, had I known that Gus offered it, and had I known that it was Randall Minning's choice. Everyone I knew wanted to be like him, needless to say. I waited for the right time to tell him how I was huddled inside Gus's Riverside Informal Tavern because of the rain, but as soon as my lab partners arrived and the rain let up we'd go back outside, cross the road to the planned Cliffs of the Saluda gated community once the workers left for the day, and pull up surveyor's stobs as part of the required field work for a class we were taking in Civil Disobedience and the Environment. Our professor "hinted" that our grades depended on such acts of nonviolence. We had already spray-painted "Recycle" on a half-dozen garbage trucks in town. I wanted to tell Randall Minning about the course, and see if he'd be willing to come in as a guest lecturer. What would my professor say if I pulled that off!

Gus said, "I don't know if they ate it or mounted it. I figure they ate it seeing as those boys don't have enough money to pay a taxidermist to mount it."

Ben Joe turned back to the conversation and said, "They didn't mount it, but they fingered it."

I laughed. I couldn't help it, and watched Randall Minning, who at least smiled and nodded. He didn't laugh out loud like I did, but it didn't seem like I was out of line.

Ben Joe slapped himself on the knee and said, "They didn't mount it, but they fingered it. They didn't mount it, but they got to play with its titties a little bit."

Randall Minning turned his massive head Ben Joe's way. "We get it. That's funny. It's quick, at least."

I quit laughing and ordered a Schlitz, even though I wasn't finished with what sweated on the table in front of me. Gus said he didn't serve Schlitz.

After a silent minute or two, Randall Minning said to Gus, "Let me use your telephone. I don't like or trust cell phones."

Gus handed over a boxy black rotary attached to a long extension. Randall Minning dialed his wife and when she answered he said, "That angel still looking down on you?"

She must've talked for a solid minute, and so loudly that some of the time we all could hear her. I wondered what the wife of Randall Minning did for a living. She had to be smart, but why would she believe in something on par with the Virgin Mary showing up in an aloe plant's fronds? She must've been that rare mixture of a person who loved and needed danger in her life, but still held hope for supernatural answers.

I secretly turned off my own cellphone so it wouldn't ring unexpectedly.

Randall Minning said, "At Gus's bar." Then he said, "Red wine." Then he said, "I won't," and "I love you," and hung up. He slid the telephone back toward Gus, who left it on the bar. Randall Minning said, "I believe Donna's smart enough to know that I'm lying through my teeth."

Ben Joe decided, evidently, that it was a good time to say, "Well at least you can be thankful that you don't have a dog's special capacity. Then you'd go home and a picture of Gus pouring bourbon would be in your pupils. Then she'd know for sure."

I watched to see if this would be the kind of response that might make Randall Minning get off his stool and shove Ben Joe's head through the broken jukebox. It wasn't plain urban myth about what he did years ago to the questionable Secretary of the Interior. He'd gotten the best of the head of the NRA, too, and then, after a few years' hiatus, that guy in charge of FEMA.

But Randall Minning shook his head in disbelief with a smile across his face. He said, "If I go home my wife's going to do what my wife always does. It will have stopped raining by then. She's going to have me start playing ball with the dog. Then she's going to ask that I go get the ladder and get a ball out of the gutter that she accidentally threw up there when I was gone. I'll say something like, 'You played ball in the rain?' and she'll say, 'Yes, I always do that when I'm afraid you're not coming back home.' And then I'll go get the ladder and retrieve the ball. Before I even think about stepping back down Donna will say, 'Hey, I got an idea. While we have the ladder out, why don't you clean out the gutters and check those shingles?' The next thing you know, somebody's redirecting the Saluda River to satisfy some rich homeowners' wants across the road, and I'm up twenty feet pulling pine needles off my roof."

Gus laughed. He said, "At first I thought it would be a good thing to have a gated community spring up right across there. Then I realized that the first thing a homeowners association will do is find a way to burn down my premises. You know what I mean? They'll talk to someone high up—a governor, or a senator who wants to play golf over there—and the next thing you know, I'm condemned."

Ben Joe got up off his stool. He veered toward Randall Minning's back and said, "I know who you are, buddy. I was pretending that I didn't, just to see how you'd act about someone not knowing you. I was playing. Maybe I, too, feel like being nice today. That's why I'm telling the truth."

Randall Minning kept looking out the back window behind Gus. The rain slackened. Randall said, "I'm just a citizen of the world, which has already been said. Diogenes said it. I don't think he ever felt like being nice, though."

Ben Joe, standing his ground, said, "You the man got us all in trouble with your talk about changing the laws about shooting rifles. You the man who wrote all those letters to the editor about changing the law so no shotgun or rifle could be fired within two miles of a church or school. They's a church or school every ten feet around here, cuz. You're ruining it for everybody."

This was all true. It had been Randall Minning's secondary campaign—behind fighting unchecked, irrational, and shortsighted land development—after a stray bullet supposedly went through his window and lodged in a three-foot-high wooden folk art carving he had on his mantel of Ronald Reagan holding a chimpanzee. If the carving had been of anyone else, the state legislature might've thought it didn't matter. If it had been a Democrat, then the legislature might pass a law saying everyone *had* to fire shotguns and thirty-ought-sixes more often. But it had been Reagan.

Actually the bullet hit the sculpture and ricocheted right up into the ceiling. Looking back on it, I realized maybe the bullet caused a leak, and then the water damage that allowed the angel to appear. Anyway, the smarter state legislators who wanted to ease a smatter of gun control into the laws used this opportunity to take a stand. And the slower legislators argued that God wouldn't want effigies of Reagan nearly splintered, even by accident. There would be a statewide referendum during the next election, supposedly.

I could see the bulge in the back of Ben Joe's waistband. He had a pistol. Or at least later on I'd say that I knew he had a pistol. But I said nothing, at this point.

Oh—and this was maybe third on Randall Minning's campaign of things to change—people said that every morning he fired up his computer and typed in "What Can I Do to Be Even More Patriotic in This, the Greatest Nation of All Time?" on Google, so that one day when the government confiscated his laptop, and when they took it into court to show how he searched things like "How to Make a Bomb" or "How to Strangle a Bureaucrat" or "How to Poison Only Government Building Water Supplies," his attorney (or Randall, should he decide again to represent himself best) would have some kind of backup yin-yang pointing in his favor.

So each day I did the same thing, though maybe to help hide other Internet vices.

"Sorry, brother," Randall Minning said. "I'm sorry that I'm of the belief that real men should do the rough work with their hands and brains, not with guns. I've lived a long time. It's how I feel. You need to eat deer? Set a trap. You need to defend yourself …"

Maybe I blinked, or looked away momentarily. Gus and I talked about it later, though, and neither of us saw Randall Minning even move an elbow, much less end up with Ben Joe's pistol gripped in his teeth, and Ben Joe off the ground a couple inches with his own belt around his neck, held up by Randall. But Gus said, "Whoa, now, let him down, Randall. We don't need this happening again," before Ben Joe could gurgle.

Randall Minning let Ben Joe's toes touch the ground. Ben Joe's face looked like it might pop. With the pistol still between his teeth sideways, Randall said, "Oh, you're a tough one, all right. I guess you think that you can talk big if and only if you have a gun at the ready, is that right? Nod your head if you think that's right."

Ben Joe quivered more than he nodded. Randall Minning let go his grip. Ben Joe collapsed—maybe melodramatically—onto the floor. Randall took the pistol out of his mouth and shoved it into his left pants pocket while pulling out from the right pocket a fold of bills held together with a paperclip. He turned to me and said, "I know what you and your buddies are up to. You'd think that I'd welcome you to the club, but in fact I'm not all that pleased. Every time one of y'all goes out trying to take on the big boys, I get the blame. Every time y'all go out and move some surveyor stakes, somebody shows up at my door wanting to compare my shoe size to the prints left in the mud. Do you understand what I'm saying?"

But he didn't wait around for me to answer, or apologize, or explain how we only did what our professor instructed us to do. Randall Minning peeled a hundred-dollar bill from his clip and placed it on the bar. He waved around his right hand in the international sign of I'll-pay-for-all-of-this. He even gestured toward poor Ben Joe's seat.

And then he left. Ben Joe got back up on the stool and said something like, "I'm going to call the cops about his stealing my forty-five," but we couldn't quite make out the words. Randall Minning walked across the road to where I meant to do the class project. I watched from the front window. The rain had stopped.

Randall Minning took out the pistol and shot out the tires of a bulldozer, kicked over a No Trespassing sign, then turned to look at us back in the bar. He laughed, then raised the pistol our way. We all hit the floor.

When the telephone rang a few minutes later, Gus reached up for it and answered. It was Donna Minning. I could hear her voice as she told Gus to tell her husband that a chunk of the ceiling had dropped. Gus said he'd go outside and do so, but I knew he wouldn't. No one would. Who was brave enough, yet, to go outside alone with Randall Minning?

We heard one more shot. No bullet came through the door or window. None of us wanted to look. What would we say if we saw that Randall Minning took his own life—that he had tired of the daily badgering, that he no longer wanted to be a Socrates-like gadfly? What would we tell a policeman, detective, or coroner? Ben Joe Purcell sat cross-legged below his stool and cried. I could've accused him of this being his fault, but taking Randall Minning's cue of forgiveness, I didn't. At least that's what I'd tell people later.

Gus said, "Well. We can't be scared down here all the time," and he walked around the counter. He looked out the window. He said, "It's OK."

Gus and Ben Joe stayed inside the bar. I crossed the road to inspect the situation. When I got there and stood between the fallen sign and the deflated bulldozer, I called out Randall Minning's name. Where had he gone? His car still sat in Gus's parking lot.

I thought to follow his trail, but there were no boot prints. I walked over to some kind of tree remover—basically a giant claw on wheels—and spit on it. I would tell my professor about that. He would ask me if I used my cell phone to videotape the entire experience, or at least to take photos. I'd say how I couldn't, how it wasn't possible there in front of Randall Minning. And I would drop the course after the professor chided me in front of the class, for doing something that he would never have the guts to try himself.

Gus opened the door to his bar and called out to me, "Look for a hole. Maybe he fell in a sinkhole from all the rain." Ben Joe came out, straddled his moped, and rode off in the direction opposite from his home. "There's got to be a hole," Gus yelled.

I stood in one place. The ground felt solid enough beneath my feet, but I scanned the area for remnants of an unexpected plunge. There were no divots or bubbles. Off behind the bar, down by the river, those two men yelled and whooped and cursed. In the distance I could hear Ben Joe's moped sputtering uphill. The wind eased where I stood, though, and an odd silence enveloped me amid the heavy machinery and surveyor's stobs. I feared moving, and thought, Can I do this for the rest of my life? Can I withstand obsession? Do I want to fight every day of my life and then disappear? Should I change my major to something like sociology or education?

A car pulled into Gus's bar. I looked over to see if my lab partners showed up. Another man the size of Randall Minning got out of the driver's side. He looked at me and held his hand straight up without waving it. Was he telling me to stop? I heard Gus say hello to the man, and ask him to come on inside. Gus walked across the road, stopped, and said it might be best we not tell anyone our story. I hoped the new arrival couldn't read anyone's pupils, like all good strays.

HUMANS BEING

THE WOMAN PROBABLY THOUGHT I hoarded things, like those sad, demented, obsessed, focused people on recent cable shows. She came to my door in search of a wild lost running dog she'd adopted from the Humane Society two days earlier, and had a drawing of the thing seeing as she hadn't had time to pull out a camera and take photos. She wasn't much of an artist. I'm no expert in all things traceable, but it seems to me she could've gotten on the Internet, Googled "dog images," found something that looked like her mixed breed, then gone around the neighborhood showing off a picture that didn't look like a crude cartoon character. I pulled the front door open hard in order to shove a box out of the way and reach my arm out to take a better look.

"A couple people down that way," the woman said, pointing with her thumb down Slaughterhouse Road, "said that you might have taken a stray dog in." She looked past my body, at all the boxes stacked up in the foyer, reaching back into the den.

"These aren't my things," I said. "These are my wife's brother's belongings. These are my ex-wife's brother's things. They're my ex-brother-in-law's boxes, I swear to God."

Her name ended up being Tabitha. Tabitha! Who's named that anymore? She said, "I'm Tabitha. The dog is about half-pit bull, half-retriever, half-shepherd, and half-chow. She's a sweetheart, and her name is Blanche. Well, when I got her at the pound her name was Stella, but I thought that I didn't want to go outside yelling 'Stella!' like that, you know, so I went with another one of Tennessee Williams's characters."

I would've bet that Tabitha took me for just an ordinary , white-trash, hoarding fool who didn't know *A Streetcar Named Desire*, and that she wanted to show off her sophomore lit skills. I said, "No dogs around here. Why didn't you name her A Negro Woman or A Mexican Woman? You could've named her Eunice, after the landlady, or Prostitute. Or you could've changed plays entirely and named her Laura Wingfield."

I thought about Gentleman Caller, but couldn't think of that character's name at the time. And I guess it wouldn't have worked anyway, what with the dog being a female.

Tabitha said, "Wow," and smiled. "You know your Tennessee Williams. I didn't think anyone around here knew anything about anything."

I said, "You can come on in here and look for Blanche, if you don't believe that I don't have her. You want a beer? It's hot outside and you look like you could use one."

Later on I would think about how Tabitha was either too trusting, or hadn't seen any of those other cable TV shows about how men will appear all vulnerable and decent, then lure dog-searching women into their hellholes.

Tabitha wore plain old blue jeans with a hole in one knee, and a T-shirt that advertised a place called Ronald's Rock and Gem Shop. She had her hair piled up on top of her head, which meant I couldn't tell if it was past her shoulders—and I had a theory that any woman over the age of thirty-seven with long hair happened to be unstable. Again, no research on the subject, just private daily utilitarian observations.

"You know what? I could use a beer," Tabitha said.

We tried to squeeze her in, and then finally I said, "Why don't you meet me at the back door? That might be easier. There's a clearer path from the back to the kitchen."

I closed the front door, and to be honest figured that by the time I got to the back Tabitha would've reconsidered and taken off running faster than stray Blanche. But when I got through my den, and down the short hall, and through the mud room where I kept all of my cleaning supplies and heavy-duty brushes, there she was, smiling, holding her odd pencil-on-paper drawing. I said, "I didn't think to introduce myself. My name's Bob. Bobby."

Tabitha walked right in. She said, "Tabitha. Good to meet you, though not under these circumstances, Bobbobby." She said, "I know, I know—my parents had a thing for that show *Bewitched*. It could've been worse. They could've named me Samantha, or Endora. Or Gladys."

She walked straight through my work room to the kitchen, as if she knew the place. Understand that this was out in the country, outside of Calloustown, not in a subdivision where all the houses had similar floor plans. Tabitha opened the refrigerator door and then the vegetable bin where I kept cans of PBR stacked rollaway-style on their sides.

I didn't tell her that my name wasn't Bobbobby.

Here's my callow story: I graduated with a degree in art history, a minor in philosophy. So it's not hard to understand that my strength is in erasing the past. Listen, one time a Chinese man was forced to clip blades of grass one by one with pinking shears for an area one foot wide by a mile in length. Someone came up to him one day and said, "Man, by the time you get to the end, all the grass behind you will have grown a foot. How can you stay so optimistic?"

The Chinese grass-cutter guy said, "It doesn't grow a foot behind me if I don't look back."

I might've made this little Chinese man story up, but that's how I looked at things. I didn't look back.

One night, drinking, I came up with this idea: There was all this news about gang members from Los Angeles and Mexico City moving into the area and graffitiing up storefronts, boxcars, parked eighteen-wheelers, houses, cars, sidewalks, asphalt roads, overpasses, river bridges, and solitary memorial landmark trees. I said to my wife, Sheila, "What if I start up a graffiti-erasing company? What a great idea!" like that. Like I said, we'd been drinking. And maybe she'd been smoking some wah-wah. At the time we'd been together as husband and wife for only a month, living in a trailer on her family's back acreage. It's a long story about how we met and married, which basically came down to "bar" and "false pregnancy." Her maiden name is "Human": Sheila Human.

I had my college degree, like I said, and Sheila worked as the secretary for a secretary for an office manager for a big-time law office run by a guy named Richard some forty miles away. She had hopes of moving up the ladder, though I doubted, even then, that she'd actually go to college, major in political science, get into law school, et cetera. Sheila could type something like three thousand words a minute, but she didn't appear to have the tenacity and ruthlessness and analytical aptitude to get through law school and end up pointing an accusing finger at judge and jury.

"You know who you should hook up with," my ex-wife Sheila said, "is this guy I met at the law office the other day. He came in to get some things notarized. He's old friends with Richard. This guy—his name's Ross—is always looking for new ideas and whatnot. He told me himself that he wanted to start up as many new companies as possible." I should've understood the overall situation when she said, "His phone number is," and then she spit it out off the top of her head.

"I ain't proud of this," I said to Tabitha there in my kitchen, "but this guy, Ross, who was my business partner, ended up running off with my wife."

Tabitha didn't look down at her wristwatch. She wore a wristwatch—I noticed, because I was looking for a wedding band—but she didn't look down at it, which I thought a person should do if she were truly looking for Blanche the Dog.

"I like Pabst Blue Ribbon," Tabitha said. "This is good beer! I used to think it was a redneck beer, but it's a good beer!" She pulled the rubber band out of her hair. It—her hair—came down to about an inch beyond her shoulders, but she had kind of a long neck so this didn't matter.

I said, "Uh-huh." I said, "Are you hot? It seems like the air conditioner isn't working."

"It's probably all those boxes in there. Boxes can act as people. You know how you get a bunch of people in the same room and it gets all hot and stuffy? I bet it works the same with inanimate objects, like boxes."

I thought, I have some things to do. I'd gotten contracted out to remove "Pollock Sucks" kind of splattered on an art supply store's exterior bricks. I thought, Maybe I made a mistake. Or maybe this is one of those things where later I can say to my children, "You won't believe how your momma and I met, and it didn't involve a bar or false pregnancy."

I got up and turned the thermostat down to about 61 degrees Fahrenheit. I said, "I'm not proud of any of this."

I found it necessary to tell Tabitha about how I called up Ross, and laid out my plans to start an anti-graffiti business, and he said "Yes, yes!" immediately, and then how he and Sheila went around at night—neither of them had any background in art or art history like I did—spray painting things around the tri-county so it looked like gang members had infiltrated the area. They spray painted "MC 13" and "Warlords" and "Hell's Angels" and "Crips" and "Bloods" and "FWMISGBSE," which stood for "Fuck Wal-Mart It Sucks Go Buy Shit Elsewhere." They did that fat-lettered, no-space-in-between graffiti that's hard to read, so that it looked authentic. It took a few months and longer, but sure enough I got phone calls seeing as I'd advertised in the Yellow Pages. "How much you charge to clean up this graffiti?" a guy who owned a pawn shop might say. "I don't suck, like they wrote on my bricks."

I told all of this to Tabitha. I hadn't told anyone about this, ever. I mean, I kept the business after Sheila ran off with Ross to Jackson Hole or some place, and I didn't go out at night to tag storefronts myself. Business had slowed down, but not that much. I'm pretty sure that some of the local dropout teenagers saw themselves as not wanting to fall behind the times and had begun tagging things themselves, wanting to act all gang-like and whatnot. Sometimes I got calls to come clean up spray-paint that read "We Rules!" or "Dixe!" or "Go Home Nigers!" Tabitha and I drank and drank, which felt good, like the old days. I said, "You can't have a dog that's half and half and half and half. That equals two dogs."

She shrugged. Tabitha said, "That makes sense."

I said, "You married?"

She said, "Let's see what's in those boxes."

Sheila has a brother named Fine. That's his name. Fine Human, that's his name, and he's a real estate agent. Fine Human! I guess before he found himself as a real estate agent and had to fill in job applications last name first, it came out "Human Fine," like some kind of citation one gets for being himself. He lived nearby, at the other end of the county, but I always saw his Human Realty signs, sometimes with "Sold!" tacked on at the bottom, when I drove around *not* creating my own graffiti to clean up later.

Two months ago he showed up in a big U-Haul truck—the biggest rentable kind—and knocked on my door. I answered and he said, "Hey, Bobby. Long time no see. Listen—how weird is this?—I was taking some shit to a mini-storage warehouse unit, and the truck broke down right here in front of your house."

I swung my door open wide because I could and said, "Hey, Fine. Hey, have you heard anything from Sheila lately?"

She'd been gone a year. I know it's bad juju and whatnot, but every day I woke up from bad dreams and then hoped that she'd gotten caught up in an avalanche with Ross, or that they broke their necks in some kind of snowboarding catastrophe, or that they ventured into Yellowstone and came across a grizzly.

Fine Human had a cell phone in his hand. He said, "I called up the U-Haul people, and they're coming right over. But listen. What I need to do is this—I need to unload my boxes. They ain't going to be able to bring me a new truck until tomorrow, or something like that. Fuckers. Is everyone a fucker, or not? So what I want to do is this—Can I put my boxes in your house, and then tomorrow I'll come over and load them up in a new truck?"

I said, "Do you need me to give you a ride anywhere? I haven't been drinking today, yet. I can take you back home or wherever."

Fine Human said, "They're sending someone over. Anyway, I need to unload the boxes, and then tomorrow I'll come over—I don't want to impose—and load them back up in the replacement truck and then take them to where I need to store them. Shit, man, me and Neely been buying too many things over the years."

I always called his wife Neely "Nearly," so it came out "Nearly Human." She taught elementary school and talked in baby talk most of the time, real squeally.

I didn't think about the situation at the time. I didn't think to say, "Why don't you just leave that truck there in front of my house overnight loaded, then transfer it over when they bring the new truck?" I didn't think to say, "What do you have in there that's worth storing, but not worth selling on eBay?"

Fine Human, ex-brother-in-law, said, "I ain't heard anything from Sheila. She just up and left, didn't she? Hey, have you seen where someone went and tagged all the cars over at Bingham New and Used Auto? You need to call up old Randy Bingham and tell him what you can do with your Taginator. Is that what you're using? Taginator? Are you using it, or Crown, or Krud Kutter, or Motsenbocker's Lift-Off Number 3, or Zep R09101?"

I wondered how he knew about all the possible products I might use. I said, "I haven't heard about Randy's problems." I said, "Yeah, let's you and me move those boxes in. If I'm not here tomorrow, I'll leave the door unlocked."

To Tabitha, drinking beer in my kitchen, I said, "That was all a couple months ago. I've tried to call Fine, but no one answered for a couple weeks, and then it came out 'The number you have dialed has been changed or disconnected.' Then I drove way out there to where he and Neely lived, but there was a For Sale sign out front from one of those other real estate agents. One of his competitors, you know. Why would anyone go through all those lies just to keep his crap in my house for free?"

Tabitha got up and opened the refrigerator. She said, "I bet that the dude who owned the car lot spray-painted his own inventory, then took the insurance money. Who's buying new and used cars in this economy? Answer—nobody. That's what he did. I read about a guy who went out every night with ice from his own ice maker, threw the cubes hard against his own hood, and then told the insurance company that a hail storm hit him. Do you think he actually used the insurance money to fix his hood? No."

I said, "I read about that guy, too," though I hadn't. I thought about what a good idea it was, to be honest, and wondered if I still had a slingshot stashed away somewhere in the house. I said, "Hey, Tabitha, where do you live, anyway?"

She looked down at her beer can and said, "'Selected as America's Best in 1893.' I'm not so sure I'd print that on my can, you know what I mean? I mean, that's kind of a long time ago. Man. That's a long time ago." She cleared her throat and sniffed.

She looked at the walls, which had nothing on them, not even a clock. "So whatever happened to the truck out front? Did you talk to those people when they came to fix or tow the bad U-Haul?"

I said, "And he never came back. Fine Human vanished kind of like my wife—or ex-wife—Sheila did. I never had his cell phone number, so I can't find him there. I don't even know if there's a phone directory for cell phones. And I've asked people around, but they have no clue. I'm talking I called the Humans— Sheila and Fine's parents—and people I knew who were friends with Fine. What I got back was either 'I don't know' or 'None of your business.' Maybe there's something in the DNA of Humans about disappearing."

Tabitha said, "Do you think I look fat in this blouse?" She sat with her legs spread apart in such a way that I could easily use my imagination.

I said, "No. No, of course not, you're not fat. Hey, do you want to call the Humane Society back and see if someone picked up Blanche?"

She said, "My ex had my name tattooed to his neck. It said 'Tabitha.' And then when we split up he had 'Ain't Shit' tattooed beneath it, in cursive. I wouldn't mind it all that much if my name were Britney or Brianna, but there aren't all that many Tabithas around here."

I said, "Is he still living around here?" I had drunk a six-pack before Tabitha showed up and I almost wanted to say, "Do you want to drive around when it gets dark and tag the Bi-Lo grocery store," but didn't.

Tabitha looked into the den where all the boxes stood stacked. She said, "Why don't you open those things up and see what's inside, Bobbobby? I'm not certain about the law, but I bet it's yours by now."

"The truck just vanished, too, before I even woke up the next morning."

Tabitha said, "I really shouldn't drink and drive. Is there any way I can talk you into driving me around to look for Blanche? Or to drive me down to Copy Roger so I can get some prints of this picture to tack onto telephone poles?"

First off, Copy Roger was about fifteen miles away. Two, it closed down right about the time the PC got invented. And how come it was OK for me to drink a couple beers and then drive around? I said, "Did you drive or walk here?"

Tabitha said, "My car's not reliable. I walked over here. I bet I walked two miles before I got here. I live over on Slickum Mill Road."

I thought, You didn't bring a leash. Wouldn't most people bring a leash along? I said, "I know that I'm a bit of a paranoid. I know that I'm not exactly Optimist Club material. So I'm thinking that maybe you're up to something. As in casing my house to see what I have."

Tabitha kept eye contact with me. She took that rubber band out of her front right pocket and wound it twice into her hair. Tabitha got up, shook her head, and opened the back door where she screamed out, "Blanche!" and then "Stella, Stella, Stella!" and then "Blanche!" a few more times.

She sat back down. I said, "I got the air conditioner on. You might want to shut the door. Listen, I'm sorry about what I said. After Sheila left, I just don't trust people in general and women in particular." I didn't mention that, in actuality, I'd been that way long before Sheila took off to a place where I hoped she got altitude sickness daily.

"No problem," Tabitha said. "Same story here. I got married, he brought me to this place, he cheated on me, and then I kicked him out. I'm kind of surprised you and I have never met before. I guess you don't ever go into town. Do you go grocery shopping all the way up in Columbia? Do you do your partying down in Myrtle Beach or Charleston?"

Here's the problem with the institution of marriage: The ceremony should require more than a two-syllable response. "I do" isn't quite enough. It's too easy to say. In order to show some commitment a husband and wife should recite something on the level of what those boys have to sing out at their bar mitzvahs. I said to Tabitha, "Partying? Really? Listen, I really haven't thought about it. I mean, I buy food and booze, but I guess I do it mostly in the middle of the day when I'm working. I'm a one-man operation. I work, and then I come back here and wait things out."

Tabitha got up to close the door. She said, "There she is. Come on in, Blanche. Come here." Her voice sounded a little like what I imagined a bovine rib bone scraped across a roller rink's surface might sound.

The dog—which sure enough looked half of about four different breeds—came in wagging her tail. Tabitha closed the door, the dog walked right up to me wagging her tail, and I said, "Goddamn." This fifty-pound dog was white, liver-spotted, gray, and black. She had the coat of a hyena, one ear that stood up, and a tail that corkscrewed upwards.

"She doesn't have fleas or anything," Tabitha said. She bent down to pat Blanche's head, and I looked down to notice that Tabitha didn't wear a brassiere. When she'd been sitting there across from me in my unobstructed kitchen I hadn't even looked below eye level, but there all bent over her loose T-shirt poofed outward and her breasts swayed.

I said, "I was saying 'Goddamn,' as in 'Goddamn I can't believe this dog really exists.' I'm sorry, Tabitha. I mean, I'm so sorry that I didn't believe you."

She straightened her back and said, "No problem. I understand."

I said, "Blanche wants you to pet her head some more."

Tabitha went to the refrigerator. She said, "How come you haven't asked me about Ronald's Rocks and Gems? Most people want to know if I'm a rock hound. I'm glad Blanche came back. I hope she doesn't run back off when I try to take her home."

I said, "I'm betting that Fine Human has a leash in one of those boxes in there. I'm betting that Fine has some rawhide chews boxed up that Blanche might like." Tabitha nodded and swallowed. I said, "Maybe your new dog ran away because she didn't like her name. Why don't we name her Tennessee, which will work for a boy or a girl, as far as I'm concerned."

The first box had nothing but wigs in it. Boxes 2 through 8 were filled with those godawful Bradford Exchange Norman Rockwell plates that don't really increase in value. Box 9 just had Bubble Wrap in it, nothing else. Boxes 10 through 14 had books in them, but every one was either about how to become a better salesman, or interesting places to see in the Rocky Mountains. Box 15 held six of those Popsicle stick baskets, which I thought were pretty cool.

"There's something wrong here," Tabitha said. "Who keeps this shit? There's something wrong here."

I worked slowly, because Tabitha bent over often and—I'll admit it—I'd not been with a woman since about a year *before* Sheila left. I said, "I keep thinking we're going to find a human hand, or an ear. You ever see that movie where there's a head in a box? I keep thinking we'll find something like that."

"I like those kinds of movies. There are more than one head-in-a-box movies," Tabitha said.

"I never answered your question. Yes. What's with Ronald's Rock and Gem Shop?"

"I dig rocks," she said. "Get it? Ha! No, truly, I used to live up in North Carolina and I found a big old gold nugget one time. This was back when gold was only something like eight hundred dollars an ounce. Anyway, I found this big nugget, and a whole lot of smaller ones, up there in a river near Rutherfordton. I kicked my husband out of the house, but I still make enough money going up there once a week or so."

I kind of listened. I stared at Tabitha's breasts, and I knew that *she knew* I stared at her breasts, and I couldn't stop.

Box 16 held a rock polisher, one of those little cylinders that spins around making plain rocks into gemstones. I said, "Wow, that's kind of weird. We were just talking about ..."

I looked up at Tabitha. She smiled. She said, "I'm thinking that you caught me. I'm thinking that you have this all figured out now."

I didn't. Degrees in art history and philosophy didn't prepare me so much for looking ahead. Like I said, I knew how to erase the past, and I knew the present OK, but looking forward seemed an impossibility. I said, "Do you want to move in here later? We could sell all this crap at a flea market, or over the internet, and then we could consolidate what we have and save some money. I don't know about you, but I've been having a hard time making ends meet without Sheila's income as a secretary to a secretary to an office manager for a big-time law office."

Tabitha took her box cutter and ripped through Boxes 17 and 18. She said, "You're sweet, Bobbobby."

We went through a box of Fine's underwear, a box of Neely's Hummel figurines, a box that held unopened bottles of hand sanitizer and some foil-wrapped condoms. There was a box of everyday plates and cups, of flatware, of middle and high school yearbooks. We came across bottles of wine, and seed packets, ashtrays, a rubber band ball, and the worst disco CDs of the seventies and eighties.

And then I said, "Ohhhhh, I get it. You were having an affair with Fine Human, and something of yours is in here. And then he and his wife took off."

Tabitha lifted her eyebrows. She sat down on the floor. "It's you and me against the Humans. Your wife took off on you, and

Fine Human made some promises to me that he didn't keep. I kicked my husband out, and he was supposed to leave his wife."

I opened up a box that held two gold pans and a sluice box. And there, in the corner, upright, was a tube of what appeared to be gold dust, or chips. Tabitha grabbed it quickly. I said, "I don't know about you, but this doesn't have your name on it, and it's in my house, and like you said, two months sitting around here means it's probably mine."

Blanche or Stella or Tennessee came up to me and touched her nose right on mine. She had the eyes of a good nun, of a grieving Appalachian widow, of a disappointed vintner. I said, "You weren't ever lost, were you, girl? You knew exactly where you were meant to be."

Tabitha said, "I'll tell you what. Let's you and me split the money for the gold. And you can do whatever you want with the rest of this shit. No, wait—I want the gold pans and the sluice. I want the polisher. And maybe two of the figurines. But you can have the rest of it."

What else could I say? I said, "I want the dog. You can have everything, but I'll take better of this dog than you will. I'll take care of this dog better than anyone, is what I'm saying."

I looked at this woman in the face and didn't smile. I could see, for once, in the future, where I'd drive around in my truck with this great dog who would be loyal and trusting. We'd cruise around the entire county, erasing what young men and women thought necessary to exclaim via Krylon to the rest of us, statements about the economy, or about their territory, or unrequited love. I would tell Tennessee to stay on the bench seat, and she would. We'd go through drive-through windows and I'd buy her hamburgers without onions or condiments, plain hot dogs, the occasional stand of french fries. I envisioned our taking a vacation together and driving to the coast where she could chase gulls and dig for whatever mollusks relished living underground.

Tabitha stood up holding what she wished to own again. She said, "Deal."

She asked if I'd drive her back home. I said I couldn't, stepped across some flattened empty boxes, and opened the front door. It's not like I wanted to be mean, but something told me that this Tabitha woman might have an accomplice hiding somewhere across the road who'd break in as soon as we left, or that she worked for the sheriff's department and could get me a DUI.

She walked out shaking her head and mumbling something. My new dog wagged her tail and—I'd put my hand on a sacred book and tell this story—exhaled a sigh that I interpreted as "Cheated Death again."

I looked out the blinds to watch Tabitha carrying her gold dust and panning utensils. She walked right down the middle of my road. I thought, Who are all these people out there who leave their belongings with ex-relatives and strangers? I thought, What brand of bolt-locks should I purchase now to make me feel safe, and what could I possibly spray-paint on my own house to scare away so many demons?